AF429254

ACCISMUS

AMBERLEE ORTIZ

COPYRIGHT © 2023 AMBERLEE ORTIZ

ALL RIGHTS RESERVED.

NO PORTION OF THIS BOOK MAY BE REPRODUCED IN ANY FORM WITHOUT PERMISSION FROM THE PUBLISHER, EXCEPT AS PERMITTED BY THE U.S COPYRIGHT LAW.

THIS IS A WORK OF FICTION. NAMES, CHARACTERS, PLACES, AND INCIDENTS EITHER ARE THE PRODUCTS OF THE AUTHOR'S IMAGINATION OR ARE USED FICTITIOUSLY. ANY RESEMBLANCE TO ACTUAL PERSONS, LIVING OR DEAD, BUSINESSES, COMPANIES, EVENTS, OR LOCALES, IS ENTIRELY COINCIDENTAL.

Formatted by Purple Fern Publishing, Fall 2023

Cover designed by Alyssa Page

Contents

FOR

the introverts; the silent dreamers…

INTRODUCTION

There are four realms in the afterlife.

Heaven.

Purgatory.

Hell.

Oblivion.

Four realms that define an individual after they die. Each realm has a ruler—be it a sole predecessor or a King and Queen. The realm you fall into has to do with choices you have made in the mortal world. When someone passes, they are immediately placed in their realm chosen by the overseer. If they were not given a decisive place in a realm, they are forced into purgatory where they await processing. If they do not fit into either heaven or hell as believed by the overseer, they are stuck in the realm of purgatory until otherwise noted by any ruler from above or below.

Then there are those born into the realms. Only high-status beings of the afterlife are given the opportunity to reproduce for the sole reason of the crown. Only a child of royal blood can continue the title of highness. Realms cannot mix. In saying this, a being from heaven cannot meddle with someone from purgatory or hell. It is forbidden and is prosecuted to the highest extent of the afterlife's laws. This is so each realm's lineage stays perfect, and each leader has clear boundaries on where their control lies—that being full control of their respected realm and its beings.

Souls are transported through the portal to their respected realm upon death. The portal is controlled by the overseer. This is the only way that those who pass on are placed in their rightful realm upon death. No one is allowed to control the portal unless instructed to by the overseer themselves. The overseer makes no mistakes, therefore where you are placed is where you were meant to be. Each realm has a running council who aids the leader(s) in law-making. Council members and members of the political system are the only ones allowed to marry into royalty, as they are members of high status. Those who are not—including citizen beings of the realm—are forbidden to meddle with royals or high-status beings of the realm.

Royal blood must adhere to strict rules of marriage, including the rule of marrying members of high status from their own realm. Members in politics and council are rotated by the overseer every ten years.

Once deceased, depending on the realm, beings are either given complete freedom of their life or are strictly bound to rules. Heaven allows its beings to live freely and happily, however that may be, if they abide by the afterlife rules stated above. Hell, in contrast, is far more punitive and stricter. Beings are controlled by the King. He has full oversight over all the realm's beings as well as say in their decision making and choices in how they live their life.

He is the only ruler in all four realms who can completely banish a soul. Once the soul is banished, they are sent to Oblivion. This realm houses beings who go against afterlife rules as well as those who have committed crimes that even the King of Hell doesn't believe to be worthy of time in Hell. Unlike Heaven, beings who are placed into Hell do not get a warm welcome. Once they are dumped through the portal gates, they are dragged by the Hill Demons to the King where they await their final sentence. Since the King has complete power, his sentence can be juvenile or extreme. It is Hell though, so even juvenile sentences are a nightmare to anyone else.

There is an exception to the rules stated above. If there is a power struggle happening upon earth that creates dissonance among society, the afterlife will become tilted. In saying this, a child will be born either from Heaven or Hell with skewed or near mortal beliefs. They will not fit into their born-into realm, rather, they are meant for the opposite. The child will not know about their flaw, as their parents may not be aware of it until the overseer calls upon them. In this instance, the parents are given a choice.

They are to have their child's marriage arranged to bind them to the realm, or they can give their child to the overseer where their memories will be erased so they have no memory of their old realm and will instead be placed into their proper realm. This child will be bound to another ruler of the opposite realm. Soulmates. It is a chain and bond that cannot be broken once the individual enters the respective realm.

CHAPTER 1

PLUMMET

"Don't you move!"

The malice laced in his tone was enough for her to look over her shoulder in protest. Her bare heels were nearly hanging off the side of the grassy platform, her eyes wild as she stood strong in her stance. She wavered ever so slightly, her body swaying as the warm breeze seemed to encourage her motive.

"Nevaeh—this isn't right!"

Her dark brown eyes danced along the line of men that stood before her, inching ever so close each second that passed by. Her father and mother among the hoard of soldiers; her nearly betrothed front and center. He continued to plead, command, rather.

"What you're doing is wrong. It's against the almighty powers and the laws created. You will not only be sinful in your own right, but also on behalf of your family and kingdom. This is not the way, Nevaeh."

Nevaeh's brows scrunched together slightly as she allowed his words to sink in, her mouth twisting in astonishment as she realized how ridiculous that sounded. She wasn't meant to serve him or anyone else for that matter. She didn't want to marry him. She didn't want to be forced into unhappiness. This was her only way out.

"You have no right to decide what's good for me. As you have no right to decide what's sinful and what is not. I'll make my own choices."

With one last look at her parents, who began to rush forward upon her words; she leaned backwards and allowed her body to fall backwards towards the blue water of the sea. She could hear her mother's wail and her father's shrill voice as he screamed her name one last time before she plunged into the cold water of the ocean below. She fought against the current, not realizing how strong the waves were. She tried her hardest to break against the waves to breathe but failed to do so, her body shaking from lack of air. She was drowning, the realization setting in quickly as she tried to fight again before her body stilled. She floated under the tides, her body looking like an elegant art piece below the raging waters above. Her body jolted slightly once and then again, as a spark of light formed under her floating body. The light transformed into a fast-spinning vortex, sucking her body into the fast-moving void.

Nevaeh had entered the portal she was hoping for when she decided to plunge toward the sea. Her pristine white wings could not stand the vortex that she slipped into, her body moving too swiftly. Usually, a member of high status moves through portals with the intention of their destination in mind. In this situation, Nevaeh's mind was not in focus to lead her in the direction she wanted. She began to panic once she realized she couldn't control her path, her wings twisting her out of control as suddenly the portal burst into a blinding mix of red and orange as she was catapulted through the regions of the afterlife. She tried to fight against the current, but it felt as if an ungodly force were pushing her somewhere else. She screamed out in frantic panic, her body getting beat down by the rapid force of movement. It was enough for her to gasp for breathable air, instead gulping down an infinite amount of salt water that burned her throat and lungs with each passing second until she gave way to gravity.

Nevaeh's body suddenly became lax as her body took a sharp plunge downward and towards a mix of fiery red and orange. The portal released her then, her rapid descent into the unknown realm both frightening and concerning as her frail body twisted in the free air downward into the smoke-filled area. Her wings were battered, bruised, and bleeding. Her condition was the same as her body, as her once pristine skin and appearance was now ragged and bloodied. In a moment's time, her body hit the ground with an alarming crack. The rust-colored earth ruptured immensely under her body, creating a gaping hole in its once leveled place. The horrific sound could be heard for miles, her weak body twitching slightly in place as it tried to bring itself to life once again but failing to do so.

Her once pristine white wings were now burned and severely broken, the remainder of them unsalvageable as the remaining feather and bone began to disintegrate to dust as Nevaeh lay nearly lifeless in the garnet-colored earth. She wheezed, unsure of how she was even alive after her journey. She blinked weakly; her vision extremely blurry before she closed her eyes in defeat. She could smell fire, smoke, even metal and—blood. She passed out then, giving into the assault instead of fighting. She was much too tired and broken to keep going, especially in her condition. She finally felt the rest setting into her bones, the slow arising peacefulness creeping into her mind as she began to accept the horrendous fact of the moment—she was dying.

CHAPTER 2

BLOOD

The black obsidian floors gleamed against the glowing fire that lined the room. The King of Hell sat on his throne with sangfroid, his green eyes cast downward at the newest damned to enter his domain.

"S-sir-please—"

"—I am your king now. You'll need to address me as such."

The quivering man looked down at the floor beneath him, tears streaming down his face as he nodded in understanding. "My mistake…King." The King's eyes narrowed now, his gaze darkening as he sensed the underlying sarcasm laced in the man's voice. "Who's King, am I?" The man's face paled more, confused by the question. "M-mine?"

"Exactly. Address me as anything other than that and you won't breathe another second. Do you understand me?"

A meek nod from the man caused the King to crack a minuscule smirk, allowing him to lean back in his chair and continue his processing.

"What is the reason that you're crying, on your knees before me this evening?"

The disgruntled man shook his head, his lips quivering uncontrollably in response, "I don't know sir—I—my King..."

The King laughed loudly then, clapping his hands together. The man immediately took in the decadent rings that lined his slender fingers. Even in the dim-lit room, they seemed to glow miraculously.

"See, now that's one of the reasons why you're here. You're a fucking liar."

"No, no I—"

"—sh sh sh. I know why you're here. It's a good enough reason, Mister Tate. You've earned your spot with the damned, that's for sure."

The bloodied man's chest rose and fell with anger, his eyes red rimmed as he suddenly became irate, "FUCK YOU! FUCK YOU, YOU FUCKING BASTARD!"

"Oh! You've got fire. I like that. Maybe I could use your ferocity in my stygian guard, or maybe even in one of the Hill Sectors. We'll find someplace suitable for you, Mr. Tate."

The King watched as his guards then grabbed the newfound damned soul's arms and legs, proceeding to carry him out and to the final processing chamber as he screamed in fear.

"Throw him in the 4th line for now. Child predators get special treatment here, Mister Tate. I do hope you enjoy the heat." The King said with a curt chuckle, taking a deep breath as the processing doors closed with an overpowering slam.

In the same moment his most trusted advisor, Medici, walked into the room through the main doors along with his sister, Davina, who wore a serious expression as she made her way towards his seated position on the throne. The guards acknowledged them both with a head bow as they stopped before The King.

"Seems you've been busy, my dearest Damien." Davina says rather sarcastically, observing Damien's rather relaxed posture as he sat upon the throne. He immediately stood tall, walking down the steps to meet Medici and his doting sister who awaited him with crossed arms.

"It seems so, my sweet sister." He replies in the same mocking tone, looking her over once before settling his hands in his pockets.

"You've been holding off this meeting, Damien. You know what needs to be done, yet you act like you know nothing of the matter. Oh, rather, you don't care." She scolds, tilting her head up at him as he rolled his eyes once before looking towards Medici who wore a neutral expression.

His green eyes danced over her features again as he gave her a slight smirk in response. Davina's brow raised immediately, clearly upset that he was taking her words as amusing rather than serious. He was always so confused as to how their personalities differed in such vast ways, yet their looks were so similar. His father would often joke that Davina was from Heaven and was just sent here to ruin the known established order—almost like a wolf in sheep's clothing. Her raven hair and blue-green eyes weren't an oddity in the hellish realm, but her seemingly kind and motherly nature was indeed. She was older than him, her brother's keeper, in a sense. Their almost ten-year age difference shows its weight in situations such as these.

"I know what I need to do, Davina. I am The King; I have other duties to attend to besides a meeting regarding whores."

Davina gasped lowly, smacking his arm in warning before pointing at him. Medici carefully grasped her wrist, giving her a look before softly pushing her hand down from Damien's chest.

"We are just concerned about your options, Damien. We want you to have time to really process this instead of rushing to choose a bride. It's better for you to handle this as priority before it's too late—"

"Enough with that. If you don't choose a queen consort soon, you know who will—" Davina continued fiercely.

"—don't mother me, Dav. I'm serious. I'll get to it when I have time. Enough of this groveling already."

Davina's features turned angry quickly, her brows tugging inward as she glared at her brother. "Enough is right, you need to do this immediately—"

"—for fucks sake—" Damien tries to speak but begins coughing harshly.

"—I don't care that you're the King, Damien. Throwing around your title doesn't mean you can escape responsibilities!"

Suddenly, Damien clutched at his neck in anguish as he gasped for air. Davina immediately stopped, her face contorting in concern as Medici did the same and grabbed his collapsing body.

"Damien?!" she shrieked, grabbing his face in a mix of fear and confusion.

His face began to bruise as his body began to blister with pain, his nose began to leak freely of blood as his eyes turned red from the immense pain of choking to breathe. Davina's screams for help alerted his fleet of the stygian guards, their presence promptly emitting a state of emergency in the castle.

"What the fuck is happening—" he nearly screamed, as he felt like his body was being burned from the inside out.

"GET THE NURSE!" Davina shouted as she held onto her brother's trembling form.

His pristine crown had been tossed on its side, its shining state standing out against the sleek black floor it rested upon. The lights seemed to grow dimmer by the second, the fire that was once ignited strongly now barely lit the large room. Davina continued to scream for help until guards came in an instant, with the royal nurses who rushed to his aide immediately.

CHAPTER 3

FIRE

Nevaeh's throat burned with such intensity that it felt as if an open flame was being placed directly upon her esophagus. Her broken limbs slowly seemed to crack back to life as she began to finally sit up from her fallen position. Her dark brown curls were matted with blood and dirt, her hand quickly shot up to rest itself against the giant wound on her head. Her once pristine white wings were a distant memory as what remained were ash and gaping wounds on her shoulder blades from their departure. The angel was disoriented, her vision unclear as she slowly looked around and took in her surroundings for the first time. Everything was consumed by fire, the putrid smell causing her to gag until she eventually retched. It smelt of smoke and blood—so much blood and burning flesh, burning metal and rust with putrid dirt. It sent her head in a whirl, her bloodied hands cradling her head as she groaned, fear settling in her broken bones as she realized where she might be.

No, please—this can't be where I am meant to be...

Suddenly, a gravelly voice broke through the screams of the environment surrounding her. Her wide brown eyes searched for the voice, her head ducking for cover as she tried to hide from it.

"We've got another in! Punch the time for processing." The voice called out, Nevaeh becoming sick just thinking about who that might be and what they might be referring to.

Her nails dug into the hot earth, the garnet-colored dirt staining her hands and nails as she squeezed her eyes closed. Maybe if she stopped moving, they would just walk straight past her frail and dying body...

"What the—hey! We've got a problem, Blaine!"

Nevaeh's eyes flew open then, immediately locking with piercing red one's opposite of her. Her breath hitched in her throat as she wanted to scream but couldn't find the strength or air to do so in this new environment. This man was terrifying. His mouth seemed to have been slashed wide open from ear to ear, now a giant scar taking its place. His eyes a deep and menacing red yet surrounded by pure blackness. His clothes were tattered, his arms adorned by a dozen scars, stitches, and burns. His hands were stained a similar red to Nevaeh's—though the color that covered his hands was much more prominent.

He held a heavy chain link in his hands, his head turning from side to side as if to admire the young woman before him.

Then, to Nevaeh's dismay, another man who looked like the one standing tall before her walked up calmly to the scene. The second man laughed maniacally, the chains he held clinking together sinisterly and almost rhythmically with the ragged screams that pierced the air around them.

"This has to be a joke. The overseer fucked up big time, huh?" The other man chuckled darkly, twirling his chain in a circle as they both began to slowly walk over to Nevaeh's decrepit body.

"Damn...the fall did a number on you, didn't it?"

"The King is going to have a field day with this one."

As soon as one of the men reached out and gripped Nevaeh's arm, she screamed out in fear. The man, in contrast, screamed for a different reason. His hand immediately began to blister, his ragged screams mixing with those around the trio as she watched in utter shock. The man gripped at his hand, his friend shouting in confusion as he suddenly looked back at the fallen angel's cowering body. His playful features suddenly turned grim as he gulped audibly.

"B-Blaine...I don't think she's just a processee —"

"—KILL THAT BITCH!" Blaine screamed in response, shaking his head in a mix of confusion and astonishment, as he stepped farther away from a cowering Nevaeh. Kane, in comparison, stood a foot away from her, watching. Nevaeh's face turned away in fear as he stumbled closer, placing his hands out in cautiousness. She slowly turned to face the scary man before her again as she tried to steady her breathing.

"Do you have a mark?"

"What?" She asked innocently, her eyes watering as she looked from the man in front of her to the furious man who stood behind him. "The Mark of Brunel. It's the royal insignia of Hell. Have you ever heard of it?"

"Of Hell?" Nevaeh croaked, fresh tears prickly her eyes as her face contorted in absolute fear and disappointment. What she had thought was true, she was indeed in the Hell realm.

"I swear to Leviathan if you don't bust her head open, I'll do it myself, Kane—" Blaine hollers before he stopped by an angered Kane.

"—this isn't a joke!" He suddenly shouts, his voice shifting deeply as the other man seemed to calm down at his outburst. Kane moves his attention back to the shaking girl in front of him.

"We can't hurt you. What is your name?"

She hesitates for a moment, but then decides to answer.

"Nevaeh."

His face fell as he then looked back to a now pale Blaine, who shook his head in disbelief.

"This is bullshit. That can't be true—"

"—why would she lie? I mean, she's scared out of her mind!"

"I don't know about this one, Kane. The King will send us both to Oblivion without a second thought if we even attempt to insult him..."

"I remember the story, Blaine. You're telling me that she doesn't look a bit out of place to you?"

Blaine looks over Nevaeh's angelic features, even covered in dirt, blood, and grime—anyone could tell she was Heaven born. Kane stays silent for a moment, then looks towards Nevaeh expectedly.

"The mark I asked about before...do you, have it?"

Nevaeh shook her head, her eyes wide as her lips parted to speak.

"I don't...I don't know what that is, I—" she began before the pain settled in. She screamed as she felt an intense burning on her skin, one she hadn't felt a moment prior. It felt as if she was being pinched by a thousand needles on the part above her heart. She carefully pulled the dirtied white silk material of her dress away from her chest to show a rather fresh-looking scar. She gasped in realization, the bloodied skin a horrifying sight as she squeezed her eyes shut. He tumbled backwards, tripping into Blaine as his suspicions were proved correct. Kane hit at Blaine repeatedly while pointing down at Nevaeh.

"She's got it. The mark, it's right above her heart."

Nevaeh had decided to keep her eyes closed, her breathing labored as she tried to deal with the burning sensation on her chest. With a long look at Kane, Blaine sighed in defeat.

"She needs to get to The Citadel as soon as possible. Call transport."

CHAPTER 4

DESTINY

DAVINA PACED THE SPACE outside of her brother's bedroom, her mind racing as she tried to calm her racing thoughts and nerves. It had been hours of hearing her brother scream in pain and agony for no known reason. He was fine one moment, but then he would digress back into intense pain. She didn't have a clue what was wrong, nor did their trusted medic and close advisor. With a rush of hot air, the door to The King's room opened as Medici exited. Davina rushed over to the man who had been tirelessly aiding her brother for hours.

"Is he alright? What happened to him?"

Medici's eyebrows furrowed as he shook his head.

"He is not poisoned, and his vitals are still essentially pure, no infections. The pain and scarring appear to be happening inconsistently. I don't want to indefinitely state a possible condition or phenomenon, rather, on his case, as I am not entirely sure if it's possible—"

"—possible? What could be possible?"

Medici looked both ways, signaling the guards to watch Damien as he began pulling Davina down the hall.

"I'll tell you, but we need to be alone." Medici and Davina nearly rushed into his office, Medici shutting the door quietly behind them as he finally turned to meet her anxious figure awaiting his medical theory.

"Just spit it out already!" She exclaimed abruptly as the man walked over to his long bookshelf, lightly tracing the many titles before gripping a very heavy and worn-out text from its snug spot in the shelf. He immediately opens it and flips through the pages, reading something over before slowly looking up to a nearly convulsing Davina. He carefully holds out the book for her to grab, his eyes trailing to the page below and to her expecting gaze before she snatches it. Medici sighs, fighting a smug smirk before speaking to her in a paternal tone.

"You should read this."

Davina rolls her eyes, turning away from him as she begins to read the words in front of her. Davina paused, her eyes moving up to meet Medici's.

"You don't mean..."

"—oh, I mean." Medici responds deeply as she moves to sit down in the chair in front of his desk, allowing the book to close in her lap with an echoing snap.

"How is that possible? We would've been alerted to a non-realm entity entry."

"No, actually, we wouldn't have. If what we suspect to be true is...then this is something that is way beyond our control. What happens from now on is by the overseer's hands and on their terms. Your brother wasn't choosing his suitor for a reason, Davina. He wasn't supposed to. It's written in the prophecy."

"Holy shit." Davina breathes, closing her eyes as she stands. She places her hands on her head and looks at Medici expectedly.

"So…now what? She's here and Damien is nearly bedridden—"

"—yes, if the idea in the prophecy stands true, she's in the realm. It would make sense how intense and substantial his wounds are and with the pain he's currently in. According to the text, the connection began as soon as she broke through the gate's portal. They're a mirror to one another, meaning if she's severely hurt, Damien is too." Medici explains as Davina springs forward to exit the study.

"The connection. We need to find her fast. Call the realm guard and have them begin a search—now!"

Medici rushes to find the realm guard as Davina continues forward and back towards her brother's room. Outside of the doors, with a small group of stygian guards, stood Dante Wentworth, her brother's best friend and army general. Dante saw Davina's frantic state, immediately sending him forward to meet her as she reached out to grasp his arms.

"We need to send a unit out to search the capital and the surrounding areas. There's been a breach in security." Davina spoke quickly, pushing Dante into action immediately.

"Absolutely, your majesty. Let's get you to a safe place—"

—no. I can stay here with my brother. We just need to find her."

"Find who?" He inquires, surprise evident in his tone as he searches Davina's eyes for an answer.

"We think…The Behemoth Prophecy."

Dante froze, his surprised expression unwavering as he stood in place before getting a harsh shove from Davina to snap out of it.

"Call them, now!"

"We need to see The King." Blaine says quickly to the guard in front of the castle's large and sinister-looking gates.

"As every other damned demand. You need to bring the soul to the processing port and go back to fulfilling your duties, hill demons."

"You don't understand, this is different. She isn't just a regular processee."

The guard looks at the two hill demons with a scowl.

"Get the fuck out of my face." The guard spits, standing tall and unwavering in his stance.

Kane finally bursts, losing his slim ounce of patience as he decides to match the guard's stubbornness with his own.

"So, you're just going to turn away your Queen, huh? Some loyal servants you are."

The guard squinted, giving the duo a confused look.

"What the hell are you talking about?"

Blaine and Kane finally stood aside, allowing the guard to see a weak and bloodied Nevaeh curled into a trembling ball on the rusted wagon held up by both hill demons. The guard shook his head in disbelief, his eyes wide as he suddenly seemed both shocked and intrigued.

"There's no way in Hell. The prophecy of Behemoth states that—"

"—that whoever holds The Mark of Brunel is the joining and rightful ruler to the realm and soulmate of the King, we know, we've heard the story plenty of times. This woman here holds the scar. It's seared right above her heart."

The guard chuckled, crossing his arms as he tried his best to hide his bubbling emotions.

"Show me then."

With frustration, Blaine growled, "Are you that stupid? We can't touch her. Just look at my fucking hand!"

The guard's face fell as he suddenly cursed under this breath, realizing that the two demons seemed out of their minds to visit the citadel if what they were saying wasn't truthful. He jumped into action as he opened the gate and immediately began to call up to the castle for aid. The royal sirens blared, the loud sound sent chills up the duo's spines as Blaine and Kane continued to grip onto the wagon and run towards the dark, gothic looking castle.

Guards followed close behind them as an emergency aid led them the rest of the way to the medical ward deep into the castle's east wing. Medici had just left the royal guard and met Davina who awaited outside her brother's room. The pair turned their heads quickly to the sound of heavy footsteps running down the hall in their direction. Medici began to rush to meet the small group, Davina following suit as her face paled at the sight before them. Medici's eyes widened in bewilderment, his hands reaching out to stop the hill demons rushing forward.

"Your highness," Both Blaine and Kane bowed their heads to Davina, only to be looked over as she rushed to look over at Nevaeh's trembling body in the rusted wagon.

"Where did you find her?" Davina asks in a rushed manner, her voice strong as her eyes danced wildly over her debilitated state.

"Near the portal entrance in Hill Sector One, your majesty. She smashed straight through, left a gaping hole in her wake. She can barely move, let alone speak."

"I can't even imagine—" Medici reaches out towards the angel, trying to better assess her wounds, before the two men shout in protest.

"Don't! Don't touch her! We learned that the hard way." Blaine stated strongly as he raised his badly burned hand with a grimace.

Medici snapped his fingers, remembering the rules he read in the prophecy immediately.

"They must touch. It's the only way to break this wicked enchantment. Once they've come into skin-to-skin contact, they should be able to heal one another. It's the first step of the bond. Get her to his chambers—" he ordered the guards, who took Nevaeh from the two demons quickly.

Davina followed the guards closely, leaving the two hill demons and Medici standing alone. They faced Medici, bowing slightly as they acknowledged him properly for the first time.

"The royal guard and the king send their warmest regard for your action this evening. Once he is well, I will tell The King of your doing. You may now go."

The two men didn't utter another word, making their way out of the castle in a hurry and back towards the hills. Medici caught up with the rest of the royal entourage, pushing the King's chamber doors wide open as the guards carefully wheeled the shaking angel further into the room and towards an unconscious Damien in the large bed fitted with black silken sheets. Nevaeh's heart rate had increased rapidly, her chest rising and falling from its intensity. Davina noticed immediately and became concerned. She nearly went into a frenzy.

"She can't breathe—why can't she breathe?!"

"She's just fine. She feels him nearby. They just need the skin to skin contact before extensive damage can be done." Medici answered quickly.

In a moment's time, Medici orders the guards to lift the angel beside the King. Before Medici finishes his order, the guards move quickly as they pick up the angel. The slim black fitting gloves which the guards wore burned intensely, a sickening sizzling sound the answer to them carrying and placing the angel on the bed beside the king.

Everyone stood back then, watching as the angel's arm had managed to land on top of the King's open palm. Miraculously, the wheezing and trembling had stopped immediately. Davina had wandered closer then, Medici following her closely as the duo was stunned into silence.

"It's...it's working," she whispered as she watched in astonishment.

As if it couldn't be more surprising, the many scars and bruises that covered the angel's body began to vanish slowly—as did the nearly identical ones that littered the King's skin. The prophecy was correct, their touch was healing to one another. The sight was a complete oddity among the royals of the hellish realm, as Davina sighed contentedly.

Medici looked her over, seeing her sway slightly. Concern flashed his features as Dante entered the room in a rush.

"Is everything okay? I see she made it." Dante spoke, his voice leveled as his eyes scanned the large bed over.

"I just need...to sit down..." Davina mumbled, her eyes fluttering before her body gave way. Dante rushed forward like the speed of light, catching her before she fell to the sleek black marble floor.

CHAPTER 5

BREATH OF LIFE

Nevaeh clutched at the black duvet under her body as she seemed to gasp back to life. Her wild brown eyes surveyed the area around her in a heightened panic, her fear bubbling upon the realization that she was lying in a bed that wasn't her own. She had thought that this was all a sick nightmare, a bad dream she would finally wake from. She did awake, though not in the place she thought. She immediately rolled over on the large plush mattress, sitting up before surveying the room around her.

The room was a mix of dark navy and black. The walls seemed infinite around her. The only thing that reminded her that this was a room were the torches of light that lit up the four corners of the room. There were also two long stretches of fire that lit the inside of the left and right walls around her. She warily peeked over the mess of black blankets on top of the bed, carefully moving to step off the bed and onto the floor.

Her breathing was now a bit shallower as she began to panic. Where am I? Her feet planted on the warm floor, her hands then moving to her clothes. The material was godly, the silk soft to the touch. The color, in contrast, made her gasp as she gripped the slip in her hands; black. She shook her head once, feeling like she was sinning already by wearing such an evil color. Black was a forbidden color in Heaven, as it was so undeniably popular in Hell. She shuffled forward, a feeling overcoming her that made her body erupt in goosebumps and her stomach to flip in anticipation. She felt almost…electrified.

As she processed this, the door to the obscenely large room opened slowly. She stopped moving entirely, her heart nearly stopping as her eyes became glued to the man who entered the room rather casually. He was handsome, she immediately thought. He was tall, taller than anyone she'd ever seen. He wore a black suit, everything down to his socks that poked through his shiny shoes. He looked dauntingly elegant. The only color he wore were his deep emerald, green eyes and matching colored cufflinks. Nevaeh immediately made note of that detail. She stepped back into the bed frame, gripping the metal as they stared at one another for a moment. There was something so haunting about him, he was most exciting to look at. His angular but sharp features accentuated him in the best way. Her eyes looked him over repeatedly, memorizing every detail as he himself looked around for a moment, a small smirk on his features as he suddenly raised his ringed fingers to his lips to wipe his amusement away.

"You alright?"

His voice—Nevaeh's stomach nearly dropped at the sound of it. It was deep, his tone like something she would hear only in her dreams. It was what she imagines velvet would sound like—dark, even. She had immediately noted how soothing it was as well, something she found odd as she knew nothing of this man and his intentions.

"Where am I?" She managed to ask; her voice breathless as the man closed his eyes in sheer amusement at her question.

"I'm pretty sure you already know the answer to that question." He countered, turning his body to fully face hers in front of the bed. He slowly began to walk towards Nevaeh, as she began to back up until she hit the wall behind her.

"C'mon. I won't bite." He started playfully, his dark green eyes shining in the dimly lit room. In response to his words, she slowly moved from the wall and took a few small steps forward. Her eyes never left his. This is such a strange feeling, she thought. The feeling nearly magnetic, pulling the young woman closer and closer to him. She was enticed, nonetheless. Then there was that palpable fear, the feeling intense in her gut. She couldn't shake it. Though that other feeling, it was brand new…what could it possibly be in a time like this—

"Do you know who I am?" He asked her casually, breaking her inner conversation with herself in an instant. His voice was deep and laced with amusement as she shook her head once in answer, unable to properly form words in her current state. She took a beat, looking at him with mock confidence as she found her voice again.

"Could you please tell me exactly where I am? There's been a big mistake."

Then it happened. The King laughed, his bright smile on display as suddenly Nevaeh drew closer. It felt as if her heart were to burst open upon seeing him react so genuinely—it caused goose bumps to erupt all over her skin. The intense feeling sent her into almost a dizzy spell, her voice the only thing able to cover her feigned interest in the mysteriously handsome stranger before her.

"—have we met before?" She inquires quickly, her voice not her own as she is entirely astonished by the situation at hand.

"Have we? I don't think that would be possible, angel."

"Why are you calling me that?"

"That is what you are, right? You never told me your name." He whispers, his head tilting in curiosity as he looks the girl over.

"My name is Nevaeh. What can I call you?"

He fakes offense, clicking his tongue before flashing a lop-sided smirk.

"Damien." He answered curtly, his smirk never leaving his angular face as he watched her become flustered the more the two stood in waiting silence.

"Well, Damien. I know I'm not home in heaven, or in purgatory because, both aren't this hot nor absolutely terrifying; nor does it have people with slashed faces and red eyes working the land." She says, her lips quivering as she became scared remembering her terrifying fall.

"Ah, you've met the hill demons— "

"—that's a fitting name, of course. Where did these said, "hill demons" take me?"

Damien's mood changed as he suddenly felt her emotion, his hands reaching out to touch her skin briefly before she pushed herself backwards at the action; his fingers missing her skin by mere inches. It was electric, a shock immediately pulsing through her body as she shouted immediately.

"Who are you?!"

"I told you already, Nevaeh."

"No, you didn't, actually. Your name means nothing to me right now. I'm in a really messed up situation right now and I need to speak with the King. He is the only one who can help me."

"You want to speak with the King of Hell?" Damien asks rhetorically, his voice raising in pitch for a comedic approach to the seemingly tall order.

"Yes, yes I do. I don't belong here, I-I was supposed to go—"

"—the overseer doesn't make mistakes in life processing, angel. You of all people should know that."

"I am not a demon, and I am definitely not a sinner. I was born in Heaven, I'm a pure soul—"

"So why were you in the portal to begin with?"

Nevaeh went to defend herself but stopped, realizing she shouldn't give so much information to someone she didn't know.

"I will tell the King once I see him. He is the only one who could possibly fix this."

"Who told you that?"

"The Law of The Three. You should know about it, being you live in one of said realms."

Damien chuckles, placing his hands behind his back as he smirked at Nevaeh.

"I know a bit about that. Though we don't really follow a lot of rules down here, so those rules kind of get…lost in translation, so to speak."

"I need to speak with your ruler, now. I can't keep wasting time."

He looked her over once, a sly smirk placing itself on his face as a mischievous glint crossed his eyes, his lips parting slightly as he watched her.

"Fine. I'm listening, then."

Nevaeh squinted, shaking her head.

"No, no, I'm sorry if I were unclear. Could you please take me to your King?"

Damien cracked a grin, releasing a deep breath. "Alright then. If you want to meet the King, so be it. Just give me a second, I can grab him for you."

Nevaeh huffed in relief, clasping her hands together as she shook them in front of her,

"Thank you, so much..."

He began to exit the large room when Nevaeh stopped him right before he exited.

"I'm sorry, Damien?"

"Hmm?" He turns, brow raised in mock concern.

"I know we kind of went over this but, if you could humor me by telling me where I am exactly?"

He nodded, clapping his hands together before raising them in the air.

"Of course, man, my manners, they just become diminished as each day passes. Ahem. Welcome to Hell. You're at the castle of his royal highness at The Citadel of the Damned." He finished carefully, seeing her face pale as a smug smile fit his face.

He had felt her fear, her heart nearly beating out of her chest as she tried her best to remain calm in front of him. He tried to sound hopeful in his delivery, possibly reassuring in a time when her anxiety was at its tipping point.

"Not to worry, though. Let me go get The King for you. I'm sure he can explain all this to you in proper detail. Just wait there."

Nevaeh nodded and stood tall, releasing a deep breath she was unaware she was holding. Her heartbeat increased steadily, her hand reaching over her heart as she rubbed the skin softly to ease her racing heart. In an instant, the doors opened again, sending Nevaeh into a shock as she stood upright in anticipation of the ruler of Hell. The warm air had pushed her curls astray, her eyes fluttering in surprise as she settled upon two men who walked into the room. One was dressed in what looked like knights' armor but not as bulky, Nevaeh noticed. He was tall and muscular, his face stoic as he looked her over once before standing off to the side of the now opened door. The other man—man? Nevaeh stepped backwards a few steps until her back hit the front of the bed. This other person…it almost looked like a creature. Eerily tall with long arms and sharp looking fingers, but entirely black from its head to its feet. A shadow, of sorts. It held a tall spear, the black gold features glimmering in the dim light of the room.

Her eyes met the floor, closing them shut briefly as she tried to calm her fear. She breathed deeply, recomposing herself as she stood tall again, realizing she would be meeting the ruler of Hell in just a moment. She stood with her hands folded in front of her as she waited in anticipation. She always wondered what he looked like. Was he as scary as her parents and teachers made him out to be? She remembers seeing sacred texts of what he might look like, devilish, and evil, with sharp teeth and red eyes. The thought sent her into a whirl as that odd feeling started to come back, the one she felt just moments ago but couldn't explain. Her tired brown eyes searched the empty doorway, her body jumping in surprise as the shadow man banged the black spear against the sleek floor twice. She cradled herself then, her body shaking involuntarily as she tried to self-soothe.

Nevaeh's shallow breath was the only thing to be heard following the loud sound. Then he entered. Damien walked in coolly, a bit of pep in his step from his inflated ego. With his hands behind his back, he walked straight up to a now pale Nevaeh who couldn't move any further backwards. Her hands gripped the metal of the bedframe until her knuckles turned a ghastly white. She gasped aloud as he stopped just a mere inch of her, his body almost towering over hers as her lips parted in absolute terror.

"Oh, angel. Why the long face?"

Nevaeh's eyes fluttered, her heart at his max speed as she saw her vision become splotchy.

"No, no..." she seemed to pant, Damien's brows tugging together before he realized what was happening.

He reached out, grabbing Nevaeh's now limp body as he groaned in frustration. He carefully laid her down on the sleek marble floor, looking down at her with his hands on his hips. He looked up and over to his king's guard, Dante, and then to one of his stygian guards. He hangs his head, rubbing his face in annoyance as he groans into his hands. He looked down at her again, almost admiring her peaceful state. Her curls wildly astray, her pink lips parted slightly, and cheeks flushed with just a touch of color. Her freckles were a prominent accessory on her dainty features, Damien caught himself staring too strongly as he pointed in Dante's general direction.

"Get Medici, would you?"

CHAPTER 6

BEHOLD

"THE PROPHECY CLEARLY STATES that a fallen angel would become part of the underworld with her name mirroring her birth realm. So, yes, she's the one."

"What does that even mean? I'm lost, honestly. Am I to bow down to her now?" Damien asks childishly as Medici shakes his head in sheer annoyance. "I'm not one for one of your irreverent tantrums now. This is serious, Damien. There is going to be a war happening between realms because of this."

"We never asked to be a part of a war and what of this war? Can't we just give her back?"

"Damien." Davina seethes sternly as he merely rolls his eyes, slinking back into his throne chair.

Damien, his trusted advisor Medici, his pragmatic sister Davina, and a quiet Dante sat in the meeting room of the castle's main wing, their new visitor causing quite a stir for them as they tried to make sense of what was currently happening.

"She's bound to the realm...and now subsequently bound to you, sir. This war...if it may come to fruition as the prophecy predicts, is because she's alien to us. It's forbidden to interact with angels, never mind marry them and make them queen. The angelic species thinks the exact same of us. It's the only law we have in common with them. Having Lady Nevaeh here...it will spark outrage amongst the more traditional damned and Hellions. They may even consider it treason by the royal hand."

Damien's brows knitted together then, his mind drifting back to the fiery angel who was way too innocent for her own good. "I don't understand how she is bound to me, yet I hadn't even known she existed before now. How can that be considered treason, especially if it's written into a thousand-year-old book I had no clue existed up until now?"

"That's the thing about soulmates, Damien." Davina replies, her tone riddled with pure annoyance by her stubborn brother.

"You never know when you're going to meet, it just happens. Why would Medici or anyone else tell you about a prophecy that may or may not be fulfilled in your lifetime? Besides, fate doesn't work on your schedule, dear brother." She continues, crossing her arms.

"You should make the transition easy on both you and the angel...this isn't something you simply give into instantly. Get to know her, try to form a bond. The rest will flow much easier when you two feel more comfortable around one another."

Medici states casually as Damien scoffs, his eyes boring into the doors of the chamber.

"Damien, she didn't ask to be here. As the king it's your duty to show her some hospitality. I mean, she is to be your Queen, like it or not. She will become your wife—" Davina begins, her voice rising the more she spoke until her brother nearly exploded.

"Enough! Enough with all of this." Damien exclaims, standing as he places his hands on his head. The tall man stormed towards the chamber doors, taking only a few steps until he was at the gold detailing of the doors due to his long legs. He was about to exit when a new voice broke through the heavy tension of the room.

"Damien, wait."

Damien's head whipped around, causing Medici and Davina to turn their heads to the voice as well. Looking rather chivalrous in his knights' attire, Dante looked towards the elites expectedly. He sighed, folding his hands on the table as he sighed.

"I think it's a good idea, man. The more you fight this, the more it's going to eat you alive. At least try and get to know her. Who knows? She may just be the one you've been waiting for."

"Don't try to patronize me, Dante. I wouldn't ever think of you to do this to me right now, I mean, seriously? You of all people should know why this shouldn't be okay and that she needs to be sent back to where she came from!" He bellows, pointing away from himself for emphasis.

"Damien—" Davina exclaims, rising out of her seat as Damien steps closer to her as a challenge.

"What? Sit down, Davina."

Davina stares at her brother angrily, her eyes like daggers as she doesn't listen to him. Instead, she raises her chin in defiance.

"I am not one of your damned, brother."

"No? I think you could've fooled me with your ferocity. I do think you forgot your place, dear sister. Since when do I take orders from you? I am your King, The King of Hell, and you? What? An extension of my power yet you hold no authority over me or anyone in this room. So, you want to talk about duties and responsibilities," he gives a curt laugh, mocking her casually as she looks up at him in anger.

"—how about you do your civil duty and stay in your fucking place." He spits lowly, watching as a single tear falls from her eye yet her face never faltered.

Damien looks at her sternly before moving his sight to a now standing Dante. The right side of his body just in front of Davina, almost as if he were ready to shield her from his venomous words or worse. Damien scoffed, knowing all too well what that meant. He decided against dropping the bomb, so to speak, and instead gave a condescending smile in response.

"I won't be made a prisoner in my own castle. That means that I will not, and will never, do something that I find unnecessary or not beneficial to myself or this realm. You speak of war like it's a small storm that'll pass in an hour or so. I find it insulting that you all would sit I front of me and suggest harboring an outlaw that will send my realm and its people to madness. Where are your heads? Medici?" Damien nearly pleads, his tone faltering in surprise as he looks wildly at his close circle.

"What the fuck has gotten into you three? Have you all forgotten how we run things around here? This isn't a walk in the fucking park."

Davina looks away from him, Dante sighing as he looks down at the sleek table below. Medici folds his hands in front of him, looking at Damien rather calmly though his tugged brows said differently.

"I won't fold. I'm not here to coddle anyone, let alone an angel who doesn't even know where she belongs. I'm not a loving man or loving husband or whatever narrative you people want to indict me with. It's not happening. If I hear about this again…let's just hope, I don't."

Medici steps forward a bit, blinking in succession before going to speak. Davina goes to interject, but he places his hand out towards her to halt her words with a look of seriousness.

"As you wish, My King. You won't hear of this again."

Damien looks over at them once more, before turning and walking towards the exit. Dante steps away from the table, his hand grazing Davina's slightly in a means of comfort before he was being beckoned by a now upset Damien. He knew this was going to be a long rest of the night.

Nevaeh's eyes fluttered open to the same room she was in before, her body aching as she tried her best to sit up. Her head was spinning, her hand claiming her curls as she squeezed gently. She groaned a bit, surveying the room before landing on new items. A brand-new gown, not as short as the one she currently wears, lay draped over the far-right side of the large bed. She carefully removed the warm blanket from her body and stood at her feet before walking over to the black satin garment. She picked it up in her hands, reveling in its soft feeling before she felt every hair stand up on her body, her hands moving to clench the gown to her chest as the room door opened without a knock.

There he stood again, Damien, The King of Hell. Nevaeh lost her ability to speak again, her throat going dry as she tried to swallow down her rising fear.

"You seem nervous, you want some water?" Damien sarcastically asks Nevaeh, who was currently on the verge of collapsing on the spot, again.

She had spoken so informally to him; she was what most people would describe as disrespectful. She had heard stories of how ruthless The King of Hell could be, mostly how he did not tolerate those who spoke ill towards him. She began to imagine the possibilities of her fate; he could probably just stick his hand in her chest and rip her heart out without a thought. He could also banish her and send her to oblivion for her harsh manner.

She closed her eyes, trying to stop her oncoming tears as she trembled in fear at the thought.

Suddenly, she jumped at the sound of laughing. The sound filled up the entire room and enveloped the space between them. Damien was floored. He was electrified by how frightened the angel was of him now that she finally knew who he was. He couldn't stop himself from laughing at how funny this whole thing was. All her fire, ferocity, and determination had evaporated in an instant.

"Where's the angel I met before? The one who was demanding she see me and help her back on her way to redemption?"

Nevaeh did her best to level her breathing, as she slowly stood tall again. She hadn't even realized she was cowering under his gaze. Damien allowed her room to breathe as he took a step back. He tilted his head at her, trying to figure her out.

"My apologies, sir, for my previous manner. It was not my intention to be demanding or rude. I am just in dire need of your help. Please, if you could forgive me."

Damien squinted, moving forward again as he leaned down just a bit so the two were face level. He stared into her eyes for a moment, suddenly feeling an odd feeling wash over him. Nevaeh had felt it again, too, though she had immediately placed it as fear.

"Apology accepted." He muttered lowly, his green eyes searching hers for something to describe this heavy feeling, before moving away and turning towards the exit.

"Change and then you're coming with me." He bellowed, prompting Nevaeh to shake her head in confusion.

"Where are we going?"

Damien looked back and furrowed his brows. "You don't get to ask a question every time I tell you something. Just get dressed. I'll be outside."

Damien had walked so quickly due to his long legs. Nevaeh found it difficult to keep up, so she found herself practically jogging behind his slender frame. After about five minutes of weaning through the winding corridors, Damien pushed open two large doors adorned with the faces of screaming individuals set in a dark gold mold. Nevaeh was startled at the sight, though she was more amazed by how Damien was able to push the heavy doors open with ease.

She stopped suddenly upon entering the room, Damien continuing his walk toward Davina and Medici who stood to the side of what Nevaeh only assumed to be the throne of the King. It was a harrowing sight, as the seat was tall and adorned with skeleton heads though it didn't appear to be bone. The skulls seemed to be cast in gold and black, some with their mouths open or without them at all. She noticed an etching of symbols along the sides of the seat, the chair and backside of it snug with what looked like onyx colored velvet. She looked down at her feet, to see dried traces of...

"...blood?" She breathed, her feet nearly giving way as she looked up at the sound of her name.

"Please, step forward." Davina spoke calmly, as Damien took a seat upon his throne.

They had watched as Nevaeh carefully stepped forward, trying her best not to trip or faint as she carefully stepped around the smeared traces of blood against the smooth marble floor. As she drew near, Davina stepped forward a bit to meet her. Nevaeh stopped suddenly, Davina offering a small smile before she slowly circled around the angel as if she were prey.

"She's not too bad on the eyes, Damien." She had said, her eyes lighting up as she was now face to face with Nevaeh. Damien, in contrast, rolled his eyes at his sister's comment.

"I'm Davina, Damien's older sister. It's nice to meet you. What is your name?"

Nevaeh nodded curtly; her eyes wide with worry as she looked up to Damien who sat coolly on the throne. He was as relaxed as ever as he casually watched her be ogled and admired.

"Nevaeh." she replied lowly, her eyes moving from person to person as she stood awkwardly.

"Don't be nervous, Nevaeh. We just have some questions, and we hope you have the answers to them, right Medici?" Davina said, trying her best to sound friendly and not authoritative as the older man finally stepped forward.

"Exactly. There is no need to be frightened. We are not here to harm you."

Nevaeh had taken a deep breath then, getting a small smile from Davina who then looked up toward Damien.

"Well, before we implore you about your arrival, we would like to see something first." Davina starts, Nevaeh swaying slightly as it was her instinct to step back, though she refrained from doing so.

"Have you ever heard of The Mark of Brunel, Nevaeh?" Medici asks, causing her to shake her head.

"Well, it seems to me that you have it, so mind explaining that?" Damien bellows suddenly, causing the three of them to look towards him in a mix of anger and surprise.

"I'm not sure what you mean…" Nevaeh begins but stops as Davina moves her hand to hover over her heart. Nevaeh's breaths are shallow as she watches Davina's actions, her brown eyes fluttering upward to meet her hazel ones.

"There, right above your heart."

Nevaeh slowly looks down at Davina's hovering hand, as she then proceeds to pull back the white silk of her dress to what seemed to be a healed burn. Brandished onto her skin, an intricate symbol which resembled a compass; a circle which had a line going down the middle with an x in its center. A star was clearly etched at the bottom of the line where it met the circle again. Davina's eyes flickered up to meet Nevaeh's startled ones again as she slowly moved back and beside Medici again.

"How were you able to travel through the portal? Only rulers of the realm or high appointed officials can do that." Medici inquired, his pointed brows furrowing as he watched Nevaeh.

"I... I don't know. I just figured I would be able to." She replied meekly, her gaze cast downward at the gold flecked floor.

Damien chuckled then, his chest shaking as he allowed his laugh to reverberate throughout the large space.

"Oh, angel. You must play us for a bunch of fools. Just tell us how you did it and why. Then I'll allow you to fly back home—"

"—Damien, *enough*." Davina spits pointedly, her eyes angry as she looked up towards her smug brother.

"As you can tell, we are quite curious as to how you made this work. We've never had an angel in this realm. For you to even be breathing right now is a sin. I'm waiting for the realm to freeze over." Medici rambles, laughing curtly as he crosses his arms with a huff.

"Honestly, I have no clue how I ended up here. My plan was to land in the Earth realm. I jumped from the highest point of my home. It's where I've seen the official portal out. I just figured...I could do it too." Nevaeh confesses, looking at Medici as he drops his arms in surprise.

"Earth? Why would you want to go there?" Davina interrupted seriously, her eyes widening slightly.

"I've read stories of that place. I never felt like I was...meant to be an Angel. Heaven isn't my real home—or so it feels. I've always felt out of place. I read that Earth is a place for everyone and everything, so I figured I could be a part of that too."

Damien's face was twisted in what seemed to be utter dismay and confusion as he listened to the wild words that fell from the fallen angel's mouth.

"Yeah so, you're telling me—wait, let me get this straight," Damien began, shaking his head as he stood and began to descend the stairs of his throne towards a slightly trembling Nevaeh.

"—you decided that you wanted to go to Earth, so you committed what sounds like suicide to leave Heaven; Heaven of all places..." Damien's eyes seemed to pop out of his head as he said this out loud, his mind unable to wrap around her ideology. He couldn't help the bewildered laugh that left his lips.

"You do know, suicide is heaven's most immoral sin? You would've been banished here once you made the decision on the spot— "

"—I wasn't trying to die— "

"—yet you jumped without knowing if you would make it through the portal. That sounds like a gamble you were willing to take." He spat; his tone cold as he walked toward her.

"I'm not a sinner." She stated strongly as Damien tilted his head, now mere inches from her face.

"Oh really? So why are you here in front of me and not on earth?" He whispered; his eyes boring into hers as she took a step back.

"That's what I'm hoping to find out. That's why I asked for you."

"Me?" he asked comically, shaking his head with a hand on his chest.

"No, I can't help you. Apparently, this whole situation is out of my hands, angel."

"Excuse me?" Nevaeh coaxed, stepping forward as Damien began to walk off.

"You're kind of like the warhead of the millennia. The key to world domination or whatever Medici was rambling on about yesterday but—you're written into the prophecy of the new world order. That's why you're here, sweetheart. I can't break what's already been bonded, as much as I wish I could."

"Bonded? What? What prophecy? Why isn't anyone trying to help me?!"

"We can't, sweetheart, it's out of our hands. That's why we were hoping you could give us insight to your arrival." Davina interjected, her face falling ever so slightly at Nevaeh's distress.

"Who can help me, then? Who do I have to see?" She nearly shouted out of fear and anger, her tears bubbling over as she quickly looked between the three individuals before her.

Medici sighed, shaking his head slightly as he then cleared his throat.

"I think you should come with me so I can explain things a bit better. Maybe if I show you the sacred text—"

"I'm not going anywhere with any of you, I don't know if I can even trust you after all of this. It's like you're trying to keep me here as a prisoner!" Nevaeh nearly sobs, freely crying as she collapses to her knees.

Damien stumbled forward a bit, seemingly against his will. He stopped abruptly, looking down at the crumpled woman before him with a wild gaze. He didn't know why he just tried to assist her, why his body reacted so quickly as it did. He shook his shoulders out, giving Medici and Davina a look before Davina spoke up strongly.

"We are not here to hurt or upset you, Nevaeh. We just want to help in the way we can. Please, come with us so we can explain to you what we know."

"No! I won't. I just want to go home." She continues, her sobs echoing through the dark chamber.

Medici slowly approaches her, kneeling in front of her as he then gives Damien a knowing look.

"Now, Nevaeh. I need you to please come with me so we can straighten all this confusion out. I know this is a scary situation, but we must set things right…"

Medici carefully reaches out, placing his hand upon her shoulder for just a second before shouting in pain. He retreated his hand to find it viciously burned, causing Davina to rush forward to his aid. He stopped her abruptly, as Neveah seemed sorrowful and bewildered at his condition. Damien looked over to a shaking Nevaeh, his face contorted in anger before Medici spoke through his pain.

"This is what we mean when we say we can't harm you. We can't even touch you without hurting ourselves."

Nevaeh shook her head, holding herself as she continued to cry.

"I'm so sorry, I don't know…what's happening to me…"

"Nothing to worry about. I can easily heal myself. Though I will need to go to my study to do this. Do you think you could join me?"

Nevaeh had slowly nodded, trying to stand on her own but she faltered. She pressed her hands against the cold marble of the ground, trying to steady her breathing as she mustered up the strength to stand. It was then that she felt a firm grip on her upper arm, which caused her to look up swiftly. Damien had reached down, claiming her arm as he carefully helped her to her feet—without an ounce of pain. The two didn't dare look away from one another, the curiosity heavily apparent in their faces as Damien didn't seem at all fazed holding her firmly.

"How?" She breathed, her voice like a steady secret between them.

His jaw clenched in response; a transparent answer not possible in the moment as he looked at the weakened angel before him.

"We should hurry. This does hurt, you know." Medici stated matter-of-factly as he began to walk with Davina towards the doors leading out of the throne room.

"Are you fine to walk on your own?" Damien asked seriously, his eyes still unwavering as Nevaeh finally dropped her gaze.

"I'll be fine." She stated, her tone wavering ever so slightly as he let her go only to grab her again when she stumbled forward.

"Just walk." He almost spat, holding onto her arm as the two walked side by side after Medici and Davina.

CHAPTER 7

APOLOGIES

"THERE. SEE? ALL IN a day's work." Medici smiled, showing Nevaeh his newly healed hand.

Nevaeh gasped in astonishment, her instinct to reach out and claim his seemingly new limb with glee. She had done so quickly and without thought, causing everyone in the room to shout. The angel carefully turned his hand over in hers, surveyed the smooth skin of his palm before looking up at Medici's wild eyes.

"I'm sorry, that's so weird of me to do— "

"—fascinating." Medici uttered instantly, claiming his right hand with his left.

"She didn't hurt you." Davina states, slowly walking over to Medici to survey his unharmed hand.

"When she initiated contact no harm was done." Medici explained and gave an encouraging smile.

"Why didn't he get burned?" Nevaeh asked quite boldly then, her question obviously about Damien.

The king chuckled then, lacing his hands together as he leaned forward on the tables.

"What is that I sense? Feigned anger? Did you want to hurt me?"

"I never said that—"

"—but it sounds like you may have wanted to."

"You don't know what I meant." she exclaimed, standing from her seat fiercely as she stared at the cool-mannered King.

"Alright, enough. Could you please be tamer, Damien?" Davina asked as she gave Nevaeh a trying smile.

Damien rolled his eyes in response and crossed his arms over his chest. Nevaeh slowly sat back down in her seat before looking over to Medici.

"You may not like the answer I give you to that question, Lady Nevaeh."

Davina looks over Nevaeh and Damien who are now having a staring match.

"Do tell her, Medici. I can't wait to see her face when you do." Damien says deeply, as he sits up and leans forward onto the table again, but now with a smug smirk.

Davina closes her eyes as she hangs her head slightly. Medici notices this but tries to stay optimistic. He clears his throat before continuing, giving a trying smile towards the nervous angel.

"Are you familiar with royal protocols, Nevaeh?"

She nods slightly, shifting in her seat a bit before answering.

"Before I... I was to be wed to a member of high status. I didn't want to—more so I couldn't bring myself to accept a life of unhappiness."

"So... If you were to marry a member of high status, that would mean that you yourself are too? That could explain why you were able to move through the portal." Davina states but is quickly tuned out when Medici speaks up.

"Only the King and Queen and appointed officials are allowed that clearance. She carries no authority in that sense, with all my respect dear." He says to Nevaeh as she nods once in acceptance.

"So, what are you then?" Damien spits, causing Davina to slam her palm on the table in frustration.

"Damien, have I not— "

"—I'm of royal lineage. The Princess of Heaven."

A pin drop could be heard in the study as everyone was awestricken. After a moment of silence, Medici cleared his throat.

"Well, that brings me to our next discussion…"

Medici takes a seat as he places his folded hands on the table.

"The reason why you didn't burn Damien."

CHAPTER 8

ACCEPTANCE

Nevaeh's ragged breaths carried her through the empty halls of the castle as she ran. She hadn't figured out where she would go but she knew she needed to leave and do it as quickly as possible. She had screamed when she realized guards were chasing after her, making her trip over her dirtied silk dress in the process. She cried out in pain, her bottom lip stinging intensely as she then tasted blood on her tongue. Unable to stop her escape now, she stood to her feet and began running again. She had realized there was a staircase leading outside so she quickly descended the steep stairs whilst looking over her shoulder. Ahead of her she saw a pathway with two large hedges on either side. She was stricken with fear, fear of what might happen if Damien or his guards caught her. The thought willed her forward into the unknown, stumbling ahead with speed she hadn't known she possessed.

She had heard voices shouting behind her to follow her into the hedge, but she could hardly hear them now. Her heart was beating so fast, she could hear it pulsate in her ears. Her chest heaved from her strain to breathe, her energy diminishing as she turned various corners with no exit in sight. She was lost in this maze, the darkness surrounding her heightening her fear even more until it took over. The fallen angel had stumbled over herself again, though this time she did not fight to stand again. Instead, she laid there and listened to her rapid heartbeat. It felt as if she couldn't breathe, the darkness overwhelming her senses completely as she closed her eyes in defeat.

She thought about what Medici had told her; she was stuck here for the rest of her life. She was to live in this sinful realm and be wed to its sinful ruler. She wasn't even supposed to be here—she was traveling to Earth. How could she be bound to a realm and person she had no choosing over? It was illegal, the highest form of treason known to demons and angels and yet—here she is. The thought tore her up inside, her chest shaking as sobs wracked her already battered body. She wailed in the darkness; her screams heard for miles as its sadness engulfed the dreadful realm.

Why? Why me? Why…., she thought sorrowfully, her frame shaking ever so slightly as she sobbed silently in the dark maze hedge.

Nevaeh had felt so much emotion at once that her body couldn't process anymore grief. She had quieted, her body a crumpled mess among the brush. She could hear only her shallow breaths as she allowed herself to slip away...slowly...sur ely...but then something had happened. It was a sound, a voice. It seemed so far away, but it called out for her. It sounded so familiar, yet she couldn't place the tone. She had heard the voice say her name once more before slipping away.

The voice calling out her name was none other than Damien, The King of Hell, the man she was ineptly running away from. With his royal guard and its highly regarded leader, Dante, following closely, Damien had continued to call out her name over and over, in hopes that she would show herself. He hadn't understood why he was even remotely worried about her or her safety, the thought never crossed his mind. Though his heart and chest were feeling much different than what his mind was telling him. It was instinctual, the thought of Nevaeh running away from him nearly set him ablaze. He couldn't understand why he felt so moved and so torn up inside at her reaction to the news. It felt almost disrespectful more than disheartening—Hell was his home. The way that she blatantly showed disgust in her response when told of her current situation made Damien sick to his stomach. *She doesn't even know me; she knows nothing of this realm enough to judge so harshly.*

Though he could internalize the fact that he is the ruler of the damned—*a sick and twisted being who gets off on hurting others and all its evil delight.* He scoffed at the memory of that statement being told to him, his jaw clenching involuntarily as he walked through the halls quickly surrounded by his guards. Dante immediately took place beside him now, his eyes focused as he tried to read his King. He knew what Damien was capable of in times like this and it wasn't pretty. Damien saw Dante's concern and almost in attempts to soothe his doubts, he spoke strongly.

"Cover all exits. I want every corner of this place searched. She may be hurt." Damien spits angrily, his fingers suddenly claiming his lower lip to find fresh blood surfacing. His brows tugged together, knowing he hadn't done anything extraneous to cause the blooming cut. He scoffs, immediately wiping it away and leaving a trace of the metallic substance smeared along his skin. He begins to descend the steep stairs of the castle leading out to the massive garden.

Dante quickly followed his hasty actions without question, his face stoic as he prepared himself for the worst. He had reached forward and grabbed the King by his forearm once they reached ground level again, prompting him to stop in his ramped search for the angel. Damien had turned with ferocity, his eyes wild and unplaceable. Only Dante could do something like this and not be torn limb by limb, he was Damien's closest friend and confidant beside Medici. Though the relationship was different. Medici mirrored a father figure for him as Dante felt more comfortable and easygoing like a brother would be.

Damien was nervous, for a reason he hadn't yet understood. Dante saw this, immediately realizing how this situation could go. He felt his body shake every second she wasn't by his side, the notion of her possibly being hurt made him sick. The look in his eyes gave him away, Dante gripping his shoulder firmly in reassurance. He had seen the look in Damien's eyes, and it made him confused though he recognized it entirely. It wasn't his place to ask questions, all he knew was that he had to be there for his brother—The King.

"We don't know what's out in the maze, Damien. We just need to be careful—"

"—I don't have time to be careful, Dante. I need to find her." Damien replied strongly, pushing past Dante's grasp hastily.

"Damien, you don't even know who she is—what damage she can do." Dante spat back just as frustrated, his fear for his safety bubbling over. It caused Damien to walk up to him so he could speak lowly.

"She can't hurt me. Trust me." Damien said sharply, his slender frame turning away from Dante once he saw the recognition in his dark eyes.

Damien moved into the darkness of the maze without another word. Dante shook his head but followed him in without another thought.

Nevaeh's brown eyes flew open as her body shot up just as quick. She had gasped for air, her lungs expanding immensely as she looked at her surroundings. She was in a bed, adorned with garnet-colored sheets. She had looked down at herself, realizing she was clean and in new clothes. She stopped for a moment, the color black standing out against her skin. She felt sick, having never worn this color before. Her parents had always told her black was a sinful color, unfit for the princess of Heaven let alone an angel. She tried to steady her breathing, her hands gripping the bed sheet as she carefully removed herself from the bed. Once on her feet, she slowly walked towards the door of the ornate room. It was a mix of dark red and black, with pops of gray accents here and there. She had never seen so much darkness in one space, the sight harrowing. She carefully reached for the door handle, pushing it open slightly to see guards standing outside. She quickly jumped back, her heart nearly jumping out of her chest as she looked around the room for another escape. Her gaze immediately landed on a large window, framed with black velvet curtains. They were almost entirely closed, shielding the outside view from her. In a mix of curiosity and desperation, she went toward the window. The angel had no time to even draw back the curtains before a deep voice interrupted her actions.

"Sleep well?"

Nevaeh had fallen forward into the small pinstriped couch that lined the base of the window's ledge, her body twisting in surprise as she looked toward the sound of the voice. Damien wore a smug smirk, trying his best not to laugh at her dramatics as he slowly walked towards her with his hands snug in his pockets.

"Don't come near me." Nevaeh sputtered, her chest rising and falling quickly as he raised his brows.

"Could you relax? You're giving me anxiety."

"I want to leave. I want to go home."

He hangs his head and groans, the sight like a young boy who just got in trouble by his mother. Nevaeh noticed this quickly, the sight making him much less scary as usual.

"What don't you understand? Medici already explained this to you. This is your home now." Damien coaxed; his voice strained as if he was speaking to a child.

"Well, I don't want it to be."

Damien shook his head, his annoyed features almost melting away as they were replaced with a grin on his face as he spoke to her.

"I don't care what you choose to believe, Angel. The fact is you can't leave. That's just the way it is."

"I'll kill myself." She shouts, causing Damien to mockingly gasp.

"Oh no! Where would you go? Enlighten me." He asks in mock shock, his hands claiming his chest in a seemingly empathetic way.

She stares at him with anger, knowing he was making fun of her and not taking her seriously. Damien's head tilts slightly as he is awaiting her answer. When she doesn't, he snaps his finger and points at her like he's come up with the greatest answer.

"That's right! You can't die if you're already in the place you'd go. See, that's because you were sent here by the overseer, who, by the way, doesn't make mistakes. So, since you're here, in my realm, I make the rules...so every time you'd wake up from killing yourself, you'd just be in the same exact spot you were in— and I would make it my business to make you suffer more than the last time you woke up. Got it?" He explains, walking closer to Nevaeh as she nearly tore the fabric of the sofa with her nails.

"What if I don't?" She spat, causing his jaw to fall slack in amazement and delight.

His lips curved upward, his smile dazzling. Nevaeh pushed the thought out of her mind as soon as it surfaced, the idea of finding him attractive made her sick to her stomach at this moment.

"I see why you didn't fit in up there in, uh… The Land of Innocence." He retorts, his teeth claiming his bottom lip briefly as he crossed his arms. He shakes his pointer finger at her, squinting as he leans down and closes the gap between them. "You've got fire…" He places his pointer finger on her lips as she visibly tensed at the action. "...but too bad for you, because I know how to handle it."

Her shallow breathing is all that could be heard in the silence between them now, her chest visibly rising and falling from the tension between them.

"How did I get here, and who dressed me?" She asked breathlessly, their eyes still unwavering from one another before he smirks in answer. He turns and walks out without another word.

She had shakily reached up to claim the skin he had touched, her lips trembling as she couldn't shake the tension from her body. She freezes up every time he is around, her body not her own. She wanted to scream at him, maybe even hit him and demand he take her home. Then she suddenly realized, *where is home?* A new voice made her jump in her spot, her heart nearly jumping out her chest from the loud sound that entered her room.

"Goooood Morning! I hope you've had a lovely sleep, but it's time for you to get on with the day!"

Nevaeh froze at the sight of a well-dressed man and a few others rushing into the room with racks of what looked to be clothes. She stood, stumbling a bit before regaining her balance. The man turned to her on his heels, clapping his hands together in excitement as he walked forward to greet her.

"Hello, gorgeous. How are you feeling?"

"I don't know, fine, I guess...who are you?"

The man laughed maniacally then, his hands quickly going up to his eyes to dab at them softly in amusement.

"Sweetheart, I'm your trusted advisor. Call me Lennox."

"I'm sorry, my advisor?

"Mhm, yes. The person who always makes sure you're on schedule and that you look fabulous while doing so. Also, you know, if you need advice."

"Why do I need you? Not to sound rude, but...I don't plan on staying here."

Lennox stops his assault on the many gowns on one of the many racks as he slowly turns to look at her. He gives a trying smile, his lace gloved hands going up in the air.

"I am so unbelievably rude, I forgot to introduce my assistant and the lovely woman who tended to you earlier this morning—Nova," the man calls expectedly, snapping his fingers quickly before motioning the person to stand beside him. The younger girl quickly fumbles with garments before handing them over to the other hand maids.

She looked to be about Nevaeh's height, short almost white, blonde hair that reached her jaw. She had a few long braids that went almost past her shoulders. She had these gentle but expressive looking eyes, Nevaeh found herself crouching a bit to reach her line of sight to get a better view before she realized how awkward it must be, so she stood tall in the same breath.

"M'Lady." Is all she uttered, her voice delicate and utterly feminine. Nevaeh went to speak directly to her, but Lennox was already three steps ahead.

"Now, now, let's get to it. I need to make sure you look absolutely stunning for the King this evening. Now, lace or velvet?" He asks, holding two sleeves of material up to Nevaeh's cheek as she draws her brows together in vexation.

"Neither, because I'm not dressing up for him."

Lennox tried to hide the shock on his face as he instead allowed a light rumble of laughter fill the otherwise silence that followed her words.

"Oh, the little jokester you are! Very cute. Now…"

He pushes the gowns down the hanger rack with ferocity, causing a loud screeching sound to be heard. It caused Nevaeh to reach up and cover her ears, her face cringing at the sound of metal on metal as Nova stood by seeming meek in comparison to Lennox.

"I see you're being indecisive, so I'll choose something gorgeous for you, instead. No worries there." Lennox says loudly over his search through the multitude of intricate gowns. He pulls one out with a large smile, Nevaeh's eyes widening at the sight before they make eye contact.

"You're going to knock the socks off with this one!"

CHAPTER 9

CONNECTION

"Shut your mouth right now." Davina nearly growls at her brother as they stand at the bottom of the main staircase.

Medici had tried his best to hide his amusement by clearing his throat, earning a look from Damien which he tried to ignore. The trio were dressed formally this evening in attempts to have dinner to welcome Nevaeh into the realm. It was all Davina's idea, of course. Damien would have much rather stood in his study and out of her way.

"This is ridiculous, really. I don't get why I must waste my time—" Damien began in an exasperated manner before being quickly cut off by his sister.

"—you have an infinite amount of time, so I cannot understand why you're acting like such an a—"

Davina was unable to finish her colorful statement due to Lennox's shrill yet pleading voice at the top of the stairs. He was out of sight, most likely still in the adjacent hall, but his voice carried far and loud as he could be heard speaking hurriedly to Nevaeh. His voice was drawing nearer, causing Davina to hit Damien on his side expectedly. He glared at her before straightening up, the guards now lining up on either side of the stairs for Nevaeh's evening debut.

"You cannot go to dinner with no jewels! You are to be Queen! You must look the part, Nevaeh!" Lennox nearly shouted before Nevaeh stumbled backwards into view.

She had snatched the bottom of her dress from Lennox's prying hands, the two still in a heated discussion as they seemed to argue with one another lowly. She was unaware of her audience below as she whisper-yelled to Lennox who was hidden from sight besides his occasional hand gestures. The guards gave the King a weird look as to which he rolled his eyes in response.

"I am not some mannequin you can dress up on whim! I am not going to wear that; I already look *ridiculous*!" Nevaeh seethed, Lennox's hands darting out with a magnificent emerald green and gold necklace that looked fit for royalty. Nevaeh pushed his hands away, her eyes wild as she nearly growled in protest.

Damien, having enough of the show, clears his throat loudly and with clear authority. The hairs on the back of Nevaeh's neck stood on end then, any color she had on her face drained in an instant as she stood frozen in her awkward leaned over stance toward Lennox. The passionate designer took this as his chance, as he quickly moved to hook the necklace in place around her neck.

"Breathe, you'll be fine." He whispers casually, before quickly speeding out of view again.

Nevaeh turns slowly then, standing tall with her cheeks pink with embarrassment as she looks down upon her audience. Davina and Medici smiled at her encouragingly as Damien wore a stoic look. He looked up at her through his thick lashes, a smug smirk on full display as she took a deep breath and did her best to avoid his gaze. She smoothed down the torso of her silk gown, the emerald green hugging her figure beautifully as she began her descent down the stairs. With each step she took, a guard would extend his hand to ensure her safe descent. Her eyes stayed cast downward, trying her hardest not to trip as she normally would. She immediately noticed how her breathing became more erratic as she drew closer to an awaiting Damien at the foot of the steps. She pressed her lips together firmly, finally making it to floor level as she lifted her gaze to be met by his piercing eyes. Her lips parted as if she were about to speak but was cut short by Davina's loud voice.

"You look divine, Nevaeh! I'm sure you're hungry so, let's get going, shall we?"

Medici and Davina began their walk towards the grand dining room arm in arm as Damien and Nevaeh stood frozen in place. She cleared her throat, fluttering her lashes in embarrassment once she realized she was staring at him oddly. Damien's eyes flickered up the stairs for a moment before landing on Nevaeh again.

"The green. Lennox's doing, I assume?"

"Clearly." Nevaeh replied mockingly, causing a genuine laugh to slip past The King's lips.

Nevaeh's blush deepened, her lips flitting upward ever so slightly as she did her best to fight an oncoming smile. Damien rolled his eyes, turning slightly as he offered her his arm. Nevaeh's eyes widened slightly at the gesture, but she slowly obliged, taking his arm carefully before they started their journey towards the dining hall.

"You're shaking." Damien mumbled, looking around casually as Nevaeh's grip involuntarily tightened on his arm.

"Yeah, sorry."

"For?"

Nevaeh looked up at him then, his gaze cast forward as she swallowed her fear.

"Sorry for shaking. I'm sure it probably unsettles you. Though I have reason to be nervous."

As soon as she finished, Damien looked over to her in astonishment. Did this mean she was finally believing what Medici told her? He remembered the look of horror on her face when Medici explained the prophecy to her. How she was bonded to Damien and this realm. That look would never leave him; it was worse than the faces he got from the damned. He never wanted to see that fear cross her saintly features ever again, and as soon as the thought came to him, he immediately promised to never tell another soul of it.

The two arrived at the hall with a welcoming greeting from the Chef and his servers. Damien nodded once in acknowledgment, walking Nevaeh over to her seat where he politely pushed her chair out for her to sit. She gave a small smile in appreciation before he left to sit at the other end of the table. Her brows knit together when she took in the dark décor of the table, the dark plum colored table sash making her curious yet nervous. She carefully reached over and carefully touched the fabric, the soft velvet material making her hum in content. The display of the table and room combined made her uneasy, the dark and rather macabre art that adorned the walls was enough to want to make her shut her eyes in discontent. She averted her eyes back down to her gold plate, a wild assortment of sinister looking vegetables and bread awaiting her onslaught. She couldn't bring herself to eat or drink anything, though her body essentially begged for her to do so.

She immediately thought of the bind rule, her eyes flittering upwards to meet Damien's; his piercing emerald, green eyes were already boring into her frame from across the table. The idea of her being trapped here arose again, drowning out the music and chatter of the table. The more she thought it back, the sadder she became. Then she began to rationalize. How would she leave? How can she get home? Would they kill her if she tried to leave?

Should I just eat?

The thought drowned out everything else, as tears threatened to spill over just as she felt a sharp pain in her head. She winced lowly, her knuckle claiming the spot between her brows as she closed her eyes in discomfort. She looked up again, across the table, to see Damien claiming the bridge of his nose in a similar fashion. Then it hit her all at once. She hazily remembers her arrival here—there was so much blood and smoke. Then there wasn't. She couldn't ever place the feeling before; she couldn't remember what had happened between her arrival in Hill Sector One to her waking up in the blue hued room. Her eyes leveled on him, her heartbeat accelerating as suddenly it became clear.

She was hurting, her body on fire, her throat on the verge of constricting fully until it wasn't, she was engulfed with warmth. Her skin that once burned with ferocity began to slowly soothe itself. Her throat becoming cool and air coming back to aid her lungs in waves. Her eyes opened ever so slightly, settling upon a blurry mess of ink and skin. She could smell him—she decided to hold her breath. She sat intensely still, her eyes never moving from him as she fought the urge to move or inhale. In a moment, he began to clear his throat, and even cough as he fought to breathe. Nevaeh gasped then, her lungs thanking her as she stood from her seat. The scraping of the chair caused everyone to stop their chatter and look over to her in concern as her red eyes looked Damien over wildly. *This can't be, how is that possible,* she thought quickly. Dante looked over to Damien and then Nevaeh again, before looking to Davina with a worried glance.

"You?" She whispered, her voice trembling as she suddenly remembered where she was. She looked down at her untouched plate and then briefly at the faces of the table. She held onto herself, closing her eyes briefly, only to allow fresh tears to fall.

"Nevaeh, are you alright?" Davina asked calmly, her hand reaching out gently as Nevaeh stepped backwards again, causing the chair to scrape further along the marble floor.

Damien stood to his feet slowly, watching her intently as she began to unsteadily walk towards the large doors of the dining room. "Don't run again, Nevaeh." He softly but strongly stated, his eyes searching her tear-filled ones as he gauged her frantic reaction.

Nevaeh finally allowed the heightened emotions to take over, her body shaking slightly as she pushed the heavy doors open and rushed out. *How could he feel what I was feeling?* Damien slowly started to round the table, not moving his eyes from the door as he rushed after her. Dante stood just as quickly, following Damien but he turned and walked backwards to talk to him.

"Don't. I've got this." He rushed out then, Dante standing idly in the middle of the room as he watched Damien leave. He locked eyes with one of the stygian soldiers in the far corner of the room, nodding once in understanding as the soldier made his way out of the dining room.

Medici and Davina exchanged defeated gazes as they, too, stood from their seated positions at the table but Dante motioned for them to stay put. "Let them be."

Neveah had managed to almost make it to the steps leading outside before she heard Damien's deep voice behind her.

"Don't run away again. I can explain whatever you need me to the best I can—"

"Did you drug me? How can you do that?" Nevaeh croaked, shaking her head in disbelief as she backed into a stone pillar.

Nevaeh gasped lowly, claiming the warm stone with her fingertips as she looked at Damien's tall figure through her cloudy vision. The frantic angel almost glowed under the warm light of the corridor, the dark night sky peeking through the end of the hall. Then she felt her chest begin to constrict and she nearly screamed because of it, turning around with ferocity to move farther away from Damien who stood just a few feet away. She placed her hands outward behind her in attempts to keep him from coming closer.

"STAY AWAY FROM ME!" She screamed, her face tear-stained and red.

Damien took one step back, clearly speechless at her outburst. His face turned serious then, as he decided to take two long strides to meet her crumbling frame. He stepped towards her with clear authority before reaching down to grab her forearms. She quickly went to push him away, but he grabbed her wrist just as did this.

"I can feel you too. So, why don't you cut the theatrics."

"Excuse me? How can you? And how dare you tell me what to do at a time like this." She spat through gritted teeth.

"It's how this works. I don't understand why or how but…it's a part of the bond. The book says it, Medici showed me. I wish I didn't have to deal with this either, okay? Do you really think I'd want to sit here and babysit an angel? I have more important things to take care of."

Nevaeh snatches her wrist from his grasp as she stumbles backward into the air of the night, the sky the deepest shade of navy possible. The air was warm and humid, the smell of smoke always apparent. Her eyes looked down and over towards the stairs behind her before she focused her sights on her wrist as she massaged the skin.

"The bond…" She whispers lowly, remembering what Medici had told her.

"Exactly why you can't burn me either if you were still wondering. We can't seem to hurt each other, well, physically anyway." he added lowly as he carefully stepped forward again.

She glares at him before closing her eyes, trying to calm her bubbling anger. He watches her as she tries to calm herself down, taking deep breaths as he clenches his fits at his side. He hated this. He hated how bratty she was being, and he hated that he had to stand here and endure it.

"Listen, If I were you, I'd head back. Davina is crazy when it comes to dinner parties, and she went out of her way to set it up so…"

Nevaeh begins to step backward, but Damien continued strongly,

"…you can hate me, despise my very existence. I truly couldn't care. Though Medici and Davina have been nothing but courteous to you. The least you can do is show them the same. I won't be going back, so don't make that decision based on me."

She stops, glaring at him with intensity as Damien allows a scoffed laugh to fall past his lips. "Why are you so upset?"

"Are you seriously asking me that? Have you lost your mind?"

"I can't read your mind, Nevaeh, but I can feel your heart beating out of your chest and its fucking with my mental." He counters, his voice strong and clearly riddled with annoyance. A part of him expected her to respond to his jagged statement, letting the banter flow as it usually does, but this time he was rewarded with silence.

He watched as Nevaeh walked past him and back towards the dining room, leaving him standing alone on the balcony corridor. He sighed, closing his eyes briefly as he felt his soldier's presence enter the space.

"Everything is fine. Just fine." He spoke rather calmly, his tone deadpan as he continued straight with his stygian solider following close behind.

Nevaeh made it back to the dining hall, walking to her seat again only to see a nonchalant Medici and Davina who were happily drinking and chatting. She tried to put on a fake smile as she was greeted by a server who offered her a drink. She tried her best to give a small, lipped smile as she shakily accepted the glass. It seemed to sparkle and had a bubbly appearance, making the dark red liquid look almost like a potion. She sighed, closing her eyes briefly as she took a generous gulp of the drink before her face scrunched immediately from the pungent but sweet taste. She coughed briefly, her tastebuds zinging as a memory hit her. It was odd but she was able to place the taste of the drink immediately. *Pomegranate.* Her mind drifted back to a time when Cassius found the otherwise forbidden fruit in a far away tree while on one of their morning courtships. He couldn't believe his eyes, neither could young Nevaeh. He had shown it to her, its deep red and waxy casing was astonishing to see up close when only seeing pictures of it in school and royal text. She wasn't supposed to, but she accepted a piece of the fruit. The two shared it under the shady tree and swore to keep it a secret between them for the rest of their lives. Nevaeh set the glass down, nostalgia and another feeling washed over her, though she couldn't place it. Instead of meddling, she tried to listen to Medici and Davina's ongoing theatrics at the table.

"You know how he is, Mister -Know-It-All. I'm surprised he even has a soulmate, being the little prick, he is." Davina laughs, downing the last bit of her drink before calling out for more.

"Now, now, Davina. You need to cut Damien some slack. It's hard being the ruler of a realm and being young while doing so."

"Aaaah, excuses, excuses. He hates the responsibility of authority but loves to abuse it. I mean, seriously, that's what pisses me off about that guy." Davina burps, her eyes crossing slightly as the server gives her another glass of the dark drink.

Medici gives a serious look to the server who looks down in response and leaves promptly.

"Now he has a wife—" Davina exclaims and motions to Nevaeh, who looks stunned at her loud voice and notion in calling her "his wife".

"—let's see if he learns how to be a man. Maybe he'll start to do things right, treat people right."

"Davina, that's enough," Medici interjects but to no avail.

"I feel so sorry for you, Nevaeh. Really, I hope that he isn't half the asshole that he is to you that he is to me."

Silence envelopes the room, the tension building until it boils over.

"I don't understand how he gets to have a soulmate and I don't."

"Davina, lovely...you've had a bit too much to drink," Medici states softly, trying to take the chute from her hand but she moves from his reach.

"He's a horrible being. The things he's done and continues to do...I deserve to be happy—not him."

"It's time to go to bed, Davina. Let's go." Medici begins, standing from his chair to prompt Davina to follow him but she rejects loudly.

"I'm not leaving! We didn't even have dessert. Look! I made sure to request the best! Where is the king? Oh, that's right, being a moody asshole as per usual! When people go out of their way for him, he steps all over them! Nothing new!" Davina is screaming now, the servers standing by idly with the trays of food before Davina smashes her glass on the table in anger.

"I HATE IT HERE!"

Medici carefully holds Davina as she collapses into his arms, sobbing uncontrollably. Nevaeh suddenly feels a wave of sadness and guilt run through her. She had no idea Davina felt this way, then again, she hardly knew her. Though she always looked so joyous and upbeat for someone who was the sister of the King of Hell. Sure, she had her moments where she was rather uncouth and mysterious, but Nevaeh didn't think of that as odd at all being she is the sister Damien. Though, more than once, she realized that Davina did seem out of place in terms of character. She was bubbly, and even courteous; traits she would have never placed onto royals of hell. She seemed...like she wasn't really from here.

"I'm sorry, I am. You must believe me, I'm so sorry." Davina repeated over and over to Nevaeh.

She kept thinking about her apology. What was she sorry for? Was she sorry for her current outburst? What about the things she said about her brother? She wasn't too sure. Then she realized something else. Was Davina apologizing about her situation? That she was doomed here for the rest of her life?... Then Nevaeh thought further. Was Davina apologizing to her for the life she was now bound to? Was she saddened by the fact that Nevaeh wouldn't have a choice in how she lived her life—sorry for her lack thereof of choices?

Nevaeh allowed silent tears to fall from her eyes, her gaze set upon both Davina and Medici before they exited the room. Medici had whispered to one of the kitchen help before leaving, as Nevaeh hadn't moved an inch and continued to stare out into the distance. The broken glass and assortment of dinner plates were long cleared along with the maroon-colored tablecloth that adorned the sleek black table. The fireplace in the distance seemed to even dim, the diminishing light in the room now mirroring Nevaeh's somber mood. It felt like forever until Medici entered the dining room again, the picture before him both beautiful and heartbreaking as Neveah sat blanketed in the moonlight at the grand table. She finally caught his eye, Medici giving a soft smile as he nodded once.

"Shall we?"

CHAPTER 10

WHEN HELL FREEZES OVER

Nevaeh hadn't gotten any sleep over the past two days. Her eyes held no shine, her face lacking any trace of life as she felt utterly trapped. Her body felt unlike her own, weak, and frail. She hadn't eaten either, afraid of possibly becoming sick or even of being poisoned by the strangers of the realm. She refused to leave her room; her legs unable to keep her upright enough to make it across the room. She felt empty, her mind and body completely numb to her surroundings. Nevaeh hadn't uttered a word either, her world becoming radio silent. There were those who tried to get her to speak, with no avail. Davina had gone to the lengths of sitting and staring at Nevaeh for hours on end. Her tactic was strong of course, to anyone who enjoyed their solitude. Davina was desperate, her actions showing that clearly as she would normally allow someone their space. Honestly, Davina felt guilty and very embarrassed for her actions just days ago at the dinner table. She knows she stepped way out of line and scared Nevaeh. She hadn't had a drink in ages, and she clearly over did it. The raven-haired woman stood outside Nevaeh's closed quarters, her fist raising slowly and then knocking softly upon the intricate gold doors.

She cleared her throat once, "Nevaeh?"

She closed her eyes briefly before carefully placing her hand on the door handle, slowly opening the door as she spoke.

"I'm coming in."

Davina was met by pure darkness, a minuscule source of light only apparent through the crack in the black velvet curtains. The yellow-orange glow of the day lit sky was the only re-minder that she wasn't just swallowed by a dark hole or worse. Davina shook the thought out of her head as she stepped for-ward towards the light, opening the curtains with a huff before turning around and surveying the room. Nevaeh lay motionless in a mess of sheets and an oversized duvet, the sight making her heartbeat quicken as she stepped forward to the end of the large bed. Her slender hands gripped at the end of the black bed frame, her knuckles turning stark white as she called out for the angel.

"Nevaeh? How are you feeling today?

Silence.

"Are you hungry? Would you like me to call for some food?"

Silence, again. Davina breathed out heavily, her lips twisting as she shook her head in frustration.

"You can't just lay here to die."

"Watch me." A strained voice rasped, Davina's heart nearly jumping out of her chest at the sound.

"Nevaeh? Hey, we've got to get you up and moving. This is not good for you at all."

Tired of not getting responses, Davina suddenly became very desperate as she gripped at one of the many sheets and began to pull it away from the bed and Nevaeh's unmoving body. She continued this until the angel lay fully uncovered. Davina rushed over to the side of the bed, worry clear in her face as she looked down at the paled woman. Her once glowing olive skin has now diminished to a sickly pale color. Under her eyes were dark sunken circles that made her look ghostly in appearance. Her once rosy lips now cracked and dry. Davina's heartbeat quickened significantly as she did the first thing that came to mind—she reached down and grabbed her arm.

Davina screamed in agony then, realization settling in as she stumbled backward and onto the ground. She continued to scream in pain, her hands now severely burned and blistering each second that passed. Nevaeh had seemed to wake from her daze, her weak limbs trying but failing to sit up and move to Davina's aid. She was desperate for help now; her voice unable to carry her need for help. Davina began to shake, the pain too severe, as she looked down at her bloodied blistering hand. Nevaeh began to plead in her mind, she called and begged for help. She had begun to call for the one person she didn't want to see. The one person she tried to stay away from all this time.

Damien had been in his study, discussing his upcoming meeting with Medici. He had felt a pang in his chest, as well as a searing sharp pain in his head—an unknown and heavy feeling washing over him. He shook it away, trying not to make a big deal of it as he took another sip from his dark liquor. He tried his best to listen to Medici, but suddenly his head began to feel heavy. It was like his brain was swimming, swelling until it burst from the immense pressure. His eyes closed tightly as he pressed the bottom of his palm to his forehead.

"Shit…" he mumbled, shaking his head in attempts to clear the pain.

He stood from his seated position, Medici following as he tried to ask the King what was wrong. Damien let out a pained groan, his head spinning.

"What is the matter, Damien? Talk to me—" Medici coaxed, grabbing the King's arms as he tried to steady him.

It was then that Damien felt an odd sensation, almost an electric buzz that coursed through his body and willed him forward, knocking into the wall before exiting his study in a haze. His eyes watered from the excruciating pain he felt, the sensation becoming more present in his body the closer he got to the source. He stopped suddenly, the pain in his head suddenly unbearable as it brought him to his knees. His eyes watered, groaning loudly as he stood to his feet again unsteadily, suddenly realizing why he would be feeling this way. *Nevaeh,* he had thought instantly, causing him to trip over himself as he raced through the halls of the castle, running towards the west wing to Nevaeh's room. He had been very moody over the course of the past week, very irritable and tired most days. He hadn't fully realized why until now. Nevaeh's absence was easy to accept, as he decided it was best for the two of them to be as far apart as possible to avoid fighting. Though now he could not shake the fear that sat in the pit of his stomach as he willed himself forward. The searing pain that he felt in his head was unbearable, his vision becoming splotchy each step he took. Though in pain, he pushed forward quickly towards her room.

Medici was not far behind him with the royal guard in tow. Damien hadn't known how quickly he could run, having never done so before in his entire lifetime. He had made it to Nevaeh's room in a flash, pushing open the doors with ferocity as he took in the scene before him.

Nevaeh lay seemingly lifeless on the king-sized bed, half of her body hanging off the right side of the mattress towards the floor. He immediately rushed forward and around the bed to throw himself on the floor with a frightened shout. Davina lay on the ground motionless, both her hands now almost unrecognizable as they were severely burned and bloodied. Nevaeh's hand was only a mere foot from Davina's body as Damien shouted for Medici. He reached down and touched Davina's sweat covered face, gently patting her paled cheeks repeatedly.

"Dav—Davina, hey. Hey, hey, hey, come on—you're alright—
"

Her eyelids fluttered briefly, before slowly opening.

"I'm here, you're alright. We're going to get you healed up, okay?" Damien spoke strongly, his hands immediately being replaced with Medici's in a frantic rush.

He hadn't even realized he had entered the room amidst his panic. Medici immediately barked orders to the guard line to pick Davina up and rush her to the medical wing. Medici grabbed Damien's shoulder strongly, looking him in his eyes.

"Davina will be okay. As for Nevaeh, you are the only one who can help her right now. Bring her to the medical wing as soon as possible."

With that, Medici and half of the guards exited the room to escort Davina. The other half of them stood strong and waited for the King's next order. His wild eyes looked over to Nevaeh's motionless body as his hand reached out slowly as he felt his heartbeat quicken again. His kneeled position on the ground gave him balance as he carefully grabbed Nevaeh's torso, carefully careening the rest of her body to the ground and into his arms. She hadn't reacted at all, his anxiety now heightened as he pushed the matted curls from her face. He squeezed her lips briefly, rocking her gently as he tried to get her to show any sign of life. He could feel her weakened pulse, his fingers gently wiping at her closed eyelids in anticipation.

"Nevaeh…Vae…" the nickname came so naturally, his hands trembled slightly as he pressed her weak body into his chest.

"Pick her up." Damien stated firmly to the guards, his voice strong and unwavering as his piercing gaze met the guard line.

Without another thought, two of the four guards stepped out of the line and reached down to grab the angel. Their gloves began to immediately burn and disintegrate on contact, their skin next as both beings held her without faltering or showing an ounce of pain. Damien stood to his feet quickly, taking the angel from their hold without another word as he walked out of the room.

Nevaeh could feel Damien's heart thud against his chest, the fast and strong rhythm reminding her of a song that she could replay over and over and never grow tired of. She felt safe in the confines of his strong arms, his warmth different from the warmth of her duvet and mattress; it was comforting. She felt like she was becoming stronger every second Damien held her close, her eyelids flitting open softly as she parted her chapped lips. Her world was hazed, the overcast light causing her to squint and retreat deeper into Damien's chest. He looked down then, nearly stopping with her in his arms upon the realization she was moving again.

"Are you okay? Can you speak?"

Nevaeh swallowed roughly; her throat abnormally dry as she tried to form a coherent word.

"Yes." She rasped, her fingers weakly gripping at the collar of Damien's silk black button down.

"You're going to be fine." He stated strongly, his piercing green eyes cast ahead as he rounded the corner to the medical wing.

His guards stopped at the entrance, only Damien and Nevaeh walking further down the corridor to the dismay of the nurses and medical staff. They immediately followed the King's hasty steps, preparing themselves for whatever he may command them to do. The duo entered the main ward where Medici and Davina were present. Davina was already mid-treatment, one hand already wrapped as Medici worked on the other. The nurses rushed toward a bed, moving the gray colored blanket down as Damien reached over to place Nevaeh down. This didn't go smoothly, as Nevaeh protested the idea entirely. She gripped at his collar roughly, his hand going to hers as he tried reassuring her. He hadn't realized but his voice wavered, fear laced in his words as he looked in her frightened and pleading eyes.

"It's alright, I won't leave." He stated as he carefully placed her on the bed.

Their once warm embrace now severed as her hands left his shirt in defeat, his body hovering over hers for just a moment before retreating to stand beside her. The nurses worked feverishly around her, prepping an IV and shouting a multitude of phrases Damien couldn't understand. One of the nurses reached down and touched her skin in the sheer adrenaline of the moment before shouting in pain. Damien couldn't react quick enough to warn them, the idea was still not normal for him to fully comprehend. It was then that one of the main nurses came forward and took charge.

"No one will touch her, it is forbidden." She stated loudly, her cohorts looking at her in bewilderment.

"Then how are we supposed to help her?" One of the nurses quipped, with nods of agreement from the others.

"We don't have the clearance for it," she says before looking at Damien.

"Well, you'll find a way. Do it. Whatever you need to do." He nearly spat in a mix of anger and frustration.

She shook her head fiercely, "I don't know how we can manage without being hurt, my Lord."

"Medici will aid you after you help her. So, help her, now!"

The nurse turned around immediately then, reaching forward to aid Nevaeh's trembling figure. Her hands moved skillfully as she cleaned Nevaeh's skin with an alcohol swab before she ordered her nurses to hold her arm down with towels as she placed the IV needle inside of Nevaeh's forearm without an ounce of searing pain in response.

"This effect won't last long; I need to work quickly and check all her vitals." She spoke out loud, shouting her needs to the women surrounding her.

It all happened so quickly; Damien watched on in amazement as he admired their ferocity in aiding Nevaeh. The main nurse dabbed a towel over her forehead where sweat began to bead, before carefully bringing a blanket over Nevaeh's body. She turned towards Damien, speaking calmly now as she bowed her head slightly.

"She should perk up in a day or so. She is extremely dehydrated. Her vitals seem fine, though it'll take her some time and a few good meals for her to get back to her usual self."

Damien nodded once, looking over to Nevaeh before he looked back at the nurse.

"Thank you, Millicent."

"Of course, My Lord. We will monitor her frequently. She should be back to normal in no time."

Medici had walked over then, nodding in acknowledgment to Millicent as she excused herself and the other nurses. Damien looked over to Davina a bed over with relief as he noticed her peacefully asleep.

"Davina is alright. She suffered severe third degree burns on both hands. It took some energy but with the spell I conjured, she should be healed up by the morning."

Damien then looked down at Nevaeh, his fingers carefully caressing the skin of her cheek as Medici watched on silently.

"Why must you do this, Damien?" Medici asks curiously, crossing his hands in front of him as he awaits his response.

"Do what?"

"Stay away...act like you feel nothing for her. What is the point in that?"

"She wants nothing to do with me or the realm deep down, look at what she's done to herself because of it. A part of me is grateful for that, grateful that she feels so repulsed by the title. It's easier this way, easier to continue to remain separate. So, I'll continue to keep my distance."

"A part of you, hm? So, what is the other part of you saying? And since when have you been so accommodating?"

"Since I was told this is how it was to be between us. I can't break what's already been bonded, but I won't force someone to be in love with me."

"Correct, though that doesn't mean it has to be miserable. You can show her that life here can be pleasant." Medici begins, only to earn a humored scoff from Damien.

"Pleasant...how could an Angel find Hell in any way-shape-or-form, a pleasant place to live?"

"She has you." Medici said confidently, his tone optimistic as he gave Damien a knowing look. "…and you never answered my question regarding that other part of you. The one that I'm certain want's nothing but to be in love with Nevaeh without fear."

He didn't dare look at Medici, in fear that his true emotions would show and make him look weak. "She can't stand to be near me, never mind be in love with me. I appreciate you trying, Medici. Though I think this union was doomed before it even began." He countered, only to have Medici look down in disappointment.

"She is frightened, Damien. She has no clue why this has happened to her, why she was chosen for a prophecy she had no clue existed...I think you should try to be more sympathetic towards how she feels. She knows nothing of this world, but that can change. It all starts with you."

Damien finally looks at Medici, who pats his shoulder reassuringly.

"Fight for her. She will come around, I'm sure of it."

CHAPTER 11

LESSONS

The castle seemed abnormally quiet over the next two days, as Damien hadn't left Nevaeh's side in the medical ward following her admission. Dante oversaw the processing of souls in his absence along with Davina who healed up the following morning as Medici stated confidently before. Damien left only to shower and in instances of emergency in terms of processing—then he was back at the angel's side in the blink of an eye. She had livened up immensely, her cheeks held its pink tinge again and her skin had regained its glowing appearance just a day later.

Medici had spelled her the first night she was admitted, to make sure she could not feign any illness or feel any instances of internal pain. Damien had believed it was Medici's enchantment and Millicent's constant supervision that made her significantly better. The pair swore it was all Damien's doing in contrast—his presence was more powerful than any potion or spell of the realm.

Damien had to leave her side regretfully this morning to discuss an important event that came up yearly for the realm. He had to make sure things were running smoothly, especially with the guest list of invitees that would attend. Medici and Davina flanked either side of the King as the trio walked the halls leading back to the medical ward later that day. Damien fixed his sleek black tie before checking his emerald cufflinks as he listened to Davina talk about the itinerary for the upcoming event.

"You must discuss the outer cities and how you're going to handle the infiltration of the newfound renegade division."

"Noted."

"You also need to be aware that this will also be Nevaeh's debut. We unfortunately couldn't have her own event as she isn't completely well, so the Black Ball will have to do."

"Lennox is already going ballistic with your coordinating attire." Medici states, trying to stifle his bubbling laughter as he looks at Davina's amused expression.

Damien tries to hide his smirk as he rolls his eyes in response, "I'm sure he is."

Before the trio step into the medical ward, Davina stops as she looks down at the itinerary in her hands. She looks up through her lashes towards Damien who turns to look at her in confusion.

"What?" He asks seriously, stepping towards her once before she looks over at Medici.

"It's the guest list. She's not coming."

Damien scoffs, rolling his head as he then squints in thought. "Why? Is she deluded?"

"Beyond." Medici interjects, as he shook his head in distaste.

"She's of high status even though she represents this new-found renegade division. It's vital she attends. Though we know there is some bad blood between the two of you…even then, business is business so it's odd that she rescinded her invitation so abruptly."

Damien sighed in frustration, claiming the area where the bridge of his nose and forehead meet in attempts to calm the oncoming headache.

"I can't bar her, nor will I beg her to attend. If she comes, I'll just have to keep her at arm's length."

"Keep Morana at arm's length? That's a funny joke." Davina mocked as Damien shrugged her off.

"That's what will happen. I don't have time for her games."

"It's weird she isn't supposedly attending…suspicious, even. She will become enraged with jealousy once she sees Nevaeh, Damien. I would take that into consideration when selecting your personal guard and security that night." Medici adds insightfully as Damien nodded once in understanding.

"Of course, I'll make sure she's accounted for at all times."

The three finally begin their way down the hallway of the medical ward to be met halfway by an elated Millicent. "She's awake! Nevaeh—she asked for you, My Lord."

Damien didn't react to her statement verbally, instead he quickly walked past her with Davina and Medici in stride. He rounded the corner to find Nevaeh sitting up in the bed with nurses surrounding her. Damien froze as he watched her move freely, placing a glass of water on the table beside her. He heard her thank the women surrounding her continuously as they bowed in response. Damien decided to make himself known as he made his entrance with commands.

"I want Lennox to prepare her clothes immediately, tell him nothing gaudy or over the top or he'll hear it from me." He states strongly to Davina who nods quickly and rushes to find Lennox.

"Medici, find Dante and let him know of Morana's lack of attendance for The Black Ball. Who knows what she's up to, I'll want him to be prepared."

"Of course."

Damien looks around then as Medici exits, leaving only his guards who look at him expectantly.

"You guys just...stay put." He says more so to himself as he turns and walks towards the small group of nurses and a wide-awake Nevaeh.

They begin to disperse once he begins walking over, leaving Nevaeh nervous in his presence. He stops beside the foot of the bed, looking at her with a ghost of a smirk on his hauntingly attractive face. Nevaeh froze, her mind going blank as she took in his appearance. His tall and slender frame looked sleek in an all-black-on-black ensemble. His green eyes looked so vibrant, even holding a playfulness she hadn't known they possessed. He looked so attractive; she couldn't help but be silenced by his overly appealing appearance.

"Hey." He said casually, which only made her shiver in response.

"Hi." She quietly responded, her voice unlike her own as she swallowed her nerves.

"How're you feeling? Medici and Milli really went all out for you." he said, carefully taking a seat at the edge of the bed as he gauged her reaction.

"I'm feeling fine. I thanked Millicent and the others; I need to do the same with Medici. They didn't have to do all that they did for me."

"No…they had to." He countered slyly, letting a smile loose as it nearly knocked the breath out of Nevaeh's lungs.

"You…well, I don't think it was required for them to go to the extent that they did. I mean, Millicent told me everything. I'm forever grateful. Indebted, even. I was being so stupid…childish…" She confessed sheepishly, shaking her head slightly as she averted her gaze and focused to pick at the fraying blanket settled upon her lap. She picked feverishly at the fabric, pulling at it with anxiety as it began to unravel under her touch.

"Yes, you were. Did you learn your lesson?" He asked a bit condescendingly, as Nevaeh's jaw went lax in surprise.

"What lesson would that be?" She retorted, her head tilting slightly as she waited for Damien's slick response.

"Being dramatic puts you nowhere but a hospital bed."

Nevaeh glared at him as he looked away, trying his hardest not to find the situation amusing.

"Where is Davina?" She asked quietly, causing him to look at her in concern.

He could tell she was afraid and concerned, so he tried to give a reassuring answer.

"She is perfectly fine. Fine enough to still be a pain in my ass."

It was Nevaeh's turn to smile in amusement, though she tried to hide it by turning her face away. Her reassurance was short-lived though, as she suddenly tugged her brows together and frowned as she remembered the reason she ended up in her current situation.

"She kept trying to help me...but I wouldn't listen. Then she...she reached down but I couldn't move I—I couldn't speak—" She sputtered, obviously becoming overwhelmed and upset as Damien stood and went to sit closer to her.

"Don't blame yourself for that. Dav was being Dav, she can't take rejection no matter what form it takes. She knew better but acted out of impulse, she knew."

"It never would've happened if I spoke up. This whole mess wouldn't have happened if I was never here to begin with."

Damien surprisingly reached out, claiming her hand carefully. His jaw jutted out as he bit back his anger, trying his best to not let his frustration bubble over. He remembered Medici's words.

"You're meant to be here, Nevaeh. Though it may be under confusing circumstances…what's meant to be, will be, right?"

"Yeah…it will be."

They look at one another for a moment, silently saying everything they desperately wanted to say with their eyes instead of out loud. Nevaeh was the first to look away, her eyes shifting down to the fraying blanket under her nimble fingertips again.

"All I do is hurt others, make them upset. I can't…begin to imagine a life where all I'm meant to do is hurt others…I just won't be able to live with myself."

Damien felt a pang in his chest at her words, his eyes shifting away from hers now as he tried not to be so reactive. He clenched his jaw, a low hum reverberating between them as a smug smirk placed its way on his face.

"Yeah, well, sometimes we don't always get a choice." He states lowly and through clenched teeth.

Her face twisted into regret in an instant, her mouth opening to rebuttal her previous statement, but Damien beat her to it.

"You aren't doing this on your own free will, Vae. It's all collateral from the bond. You said it yourself. You didn't mean to come here; you had no clue a prophecy even existed. Therefore, you really have no control over its repercussions."

"Vae?" She repeated, her tone soft as she realized what he had called her.

He closed his eyes for a minute, upset at himself for saying it so nonchalantly. It came so naturally, though. It was almost as if it was meant for him to say, a name only he called her. It was almost intimate, a secret only they shared. Her heartbeat rapidly increased, a shy blush creeping onto her cheeks as she looked at him bashfully. Damien sat silently, not looking at her as he hoped she would let it go.

"You had called me that before, too, didn't you?"

He had stood then, buttoning his fitted suit jacket before placing his hands in his pockets again. Ignoring her question, he looks at her expectedly. He cleared his throat, motioning towards the exit.

"So, are you going to keep acting crippled or are you going to leave with me?"

"We aren't leaving until you finish." Damien stated matter-of-factly as he didn't look up from the book in his grasp.

Nevaeh sighed, trying her best to find the food in front of her appetizing.

"I can't."

"So, I guess we'll both sit at this table for eternity...because you're not getting up until you eat." He replies, his focus still on the pages in front of him.

In a fit of disobedience, Nevaeh stands from her seat with an amused grin. Damien pauses and finally looks up from the book, standing as well. He towers over her, causing her amused smirk to turn down as she looks up at him.

"Are you testing me?" He softly but playfully inquired.

Nevaeh shook her head no but answered the oppositely.

"Absolutely."

Confused herself, her eyes widened as Damien squinted.

"You seem confused. Do I make you nervous?"

"What would bring you to that conclusion?" She spat quickly.

"Your mind," he softly presses his index finger against her forehead.

"...is saying something different..." he carefully and slowly traces his finger down to her lips.

"...from your mouth." Damien traces her lips briefly before raising a brow at her dazed expression.

"I was just making sure you were keeping up." She mused, trying her best to sound confident but her voice came out breathless.

He smirked smugly, leaning down so he could talk into her ear. Nevaeh closed her eyes at the action, her body on fire even with the small gesture.

"Sit." he said sternly, grazing his lips over the shell of her ear before she forced herself back into her chair.

With an apparent blush across her face, she averted his gaze as she focused on the food in front of her. She didn't want a heavy meal, so Damien had ordered his chef to prepare an oversized charcuterie platter filled with an assortment of fruits, vegetables, and breads. Though these options looked sinister, almost like they'd fight back if she touched them. The vegetables had a spiky appearance while the fruits came in a hodgepodge of different reds. The bread was the only normal looking item on the plate. Nevaeh picked up her fork and went for a maroon-colored fruit that looked like a strawberry without the leafy top. She raised it towards her mouth, her face twisting as Damien pretended not to pay her any attention.

"Damien, please…" she began suddenly, dropping the untouched fruit and fork to her plate with a loud clatter. Her eyes pleaded with him, the sight almost causing Damien to short-circuit at the sound of his name leaving her lips in such a desperate manner.

"What?" He spat, his unplaced and overwhelming feelings getting the best of him.

"Look, I'm really not hungry."

"Milli said you must eat. No skipping meals."

"This isn't even a meal," she mumbles under her breath like a child, causing Damien to place his book down in a mix of annoyance and frustration.

"Speak up."

"This isn't a meal, so what's the point?" she replied stubbornly.

"You said you didn't want something heavy, so this is what you get."

"Sure, though I would like something edible at least. I didn't know that was such a harrowing job to do." She retorts and his eyes widen at how feisty she's suddenly being.

"Okay *princess*," he begins sarcastically, standing and walking around to her before grabbing her chair and pushing it out so he can lean in towards her.

"…what would you like then, for the *last* and *final* time?"

Damien couldn't imagine what Nevaeh would say next. He had found himself standing with crossed arms in the castle's kitchen, watching the angel as she greedily ate an assortment of dessert back-to-back. First it was a decadent slice of red velvet cake, and then some fudge filled pastries, now she was taking fresh dark chocolate cookies off a now cooled baking sheet.

"Hey, I know Gluttony. I can tell him he has competition."

Nevaeh gave him a spiteful look, before finishing off the cookie.

"I'd rather be gluttonous than angry."

"Are you saying I'm angry?"

"You're always angry."

"No, I'm not."

"That's what angry people say when you tell them they're always angry."

"Were you this talkative and combative upstairs? Is that why they kicked you out?"

"I left on my own terms, no one kicked me out."

"Oh, that's right. You tried killing yourself. Makes sense, being that you ended up here."

Nevaeh glared at him, crossing her arms before continuing.

"I honestly still don't understand my reason for even being here. I get a prophecy but like…why me specifically?"

"It was written long before you and I were even a thought."

"Why? Why was it written and why us?"

Damien shrugged nonchalantly before his brows tugged together as he thought about her question. "That's something I wish I knew. Only the overseer would have the answer for that."

Nevaeh shakes her head, beginning to walk out of the kitchen and into the hall with Damien on her heels. "Doesn't that bother you? How much this said power—the overseer—holds, yet no one knows who they are? I mean, when was the last time someone saw this person. What if they aren't even a person at all?" She rambled, her head starting to throb just a bit.

"You question a lot for someone who's never seen much of anything."

"Isn't that the point? Why believe everything you're told?"

Nevaeh turns then, standing a bit too close for comfort to Damien who tries his best to hide his oncoming smirk. She slowly steps back a bit, allowing space for her to look at him.

"The more I talk to you, the more I think I understand why you're here…" he says rather lowly, stepping closely to Nevaeh as he locked eyes with her. He then looked up towards the ceiling, giving his next words more direction.

"—and not up there."

"Heaven is a beautiful place, but that doesn't mean it's perfect. There were rules and regulations I didn't understand or agree with. You know, like me having to marry someone based solely on their status. Cassius is a good man; he is one of my great friends. Though I couldn't see myself marrying him. I am not in love with him in that way. Why should I be forced into a union which is already doomed with unhappiness from the start?"

Damien nods, his hands finding his pockets as he looks down at the thinking angel.

"I hated the idea of tying myself to a choice or even a person I couldn't choose in the first place. That's why I wanted to…why I wanted to go to Earth. It's the realm of free will, of endless possibilities. I've read so much of that place…it somehow, oddly, feels like home. Rather, I could make it my home."

Damien raises a brow, crossing his arms as he steps away from her and begins walking. She follows suit easily. "Earth isn't all sunshine and roses, Neveah. If you've read enough, you should know that." He counters rather inquisitively.

"Not the Earth I read about." She replies defensively, mirroring his posture as she crosses her arms too.

He chuckles, letting his arms loose as his hands find a home in his pant pockets.

"You know, you're more than welcome to do research in my study. Every book you have yet to read is there. Maybe you should learn more about the Earth realm before you trip up and learn your lesson the hard way."

"Is that a threat?" She almost gasped, her eyes wild as they searched his piercing ones for an honest answer.

"Take it as you please. Though, one thing to know about me…" he starts, slowing his steps before stopping at the balcony ledge, leaning besides it as she walks to stand next to him before she looks at him in anticipation. He leans forward slightly, a tactic to make her nervous as Neveah had come to notice.

"…I state my threats directly. It thrills me to see the fear in someone's eyes once they register my intentions."

Neveah stared him down for what seemed like ages, but it only lasted a moment before she turned and looked outwards to the city below them.

"It's hauntingly beautiful. Scary looking but, there's always beauty in madness."

Damien turned to lean over the balcony's edge, looking at the picturesque scene of the city before nodding in quick succession.

"It's something."

CHAPTER 12

QUESTIONS

Damien was absent for the following few days, leaving Ne-veah in the hands of Lennox and Davina. The Angel stood on top of a pedestal in Lennox's studio, his crazy eyes taking in every measurement and feature of her frame as he hastily sketched and took notes in his notebook.

"Is all this truly necessary? I mean, it's just a party, right?"

Lennox stopped cold in his sketching to look up at Nevaeh in mock horror.

"Please, dear, do not ever disrespect my process ever again."

He stands, snatching his tape from his shoulder and pulling it around Neveah's waist. Nevaeh stood quiet as she allowed Lennox's nimble fingers to work.

"What is this event, The Black Ball? Davina mentioned it occurs every year."

"Yes, it does. It's something of a grand town meeting. All the realms' division leaders and high-status members meet at the castle to discuss politics and social guidelines. Usually it's more partying than anything, being that Damien always keeps the realms habitants in line."

"I didn't know there were divisions. You mean, like, cities?"

"Mhm. There are three cities outside the royal grounds. They were originally meant to be two, where each city harbored souls who committed specific sins. Though with time it became quite muddy. A lot of times souls who were banished to hell committed more than one of the city's sin guidelines. So, Satan had created another city where these damned souls could be kept."

"I had no idea. My parents always made it seem like it was just a chaotic free-for all here."

"Oh, no. Even us Hellions need some structure. Damien does a swell job at that. He makes his father proud."

Neveah tilts her head at Lennox, who turns his back to her to gather some silk.

"His...father. Satan?" she asks, rhetorically.

Lennox turns, his face blank as he thought she would have known all this already.

"Yes."

"What about his mother?"

Lennox allows himself to sigh, smiling to himself as he etches some measurements onto the red silk below him.

"Danica. She was the most beautiful woman in all the realm, her kind heart unnatural for such a wicked place."

"She wasn't evil?"

Lennox scoffed, raising some different colored silk pieces to Neveah's face.

"Far from it."

"Where are they? Did they...die?"

Lennox stops then, giving her a reassuring smile as he turns back to his worktable.

"You should be asking your king about these things. They are personal to him; I shouldn't have even taken the conversation this far."

"Sorry, it's just...it's difficult talking to him. I feel like all we do is disagree."

"You both will come around. This whole thing is new for you, as it is for him. He isn't used to having someone so pure hearted as you are around."

Neveah walked around the castle alone later that day, admiring the tall structures and gold detailing of the walls. The sky was now turning a navy shade of blue from its previous red-orange cast. She admired the deep color, carrying herself to the outdoor balcony which led to the garden she ran into the second day she was here. She slowly made her way down the steep steps, the memory of her running for her life and the fear she felt making her chest constrict. Unknown to her, Damien had just finished his processing for the evening and caught sight of her descending the stairs of the castle. He had stopped, watching her as Dante and the guards followed his actions.

"Déjà vu, huh." Dante stated, his eyes cast on Damien as he watched Neveah slowly look around until her eyes locked with his.

They held each other's gaze for a moment before he began to walk down the steps to meet her. "Notify Medici of what we discussed. We will regroup in the morning." Damien continued, his eyes never leaving hers as she tried to hide her sheepish grin. When he finally made it to ground level, he cleared his throat and pushed his hands in his pockets.

"It's dangerous to wander off at night by yourself."

"Dangerous for who? Certainly not me."

Damien's head shook in mock surprise and humor, as he watched her turn her back to him and continue into the garden hedge. The walkway through the garden's maze was now illuminated, pillars with bright flames lighting the way for the two to walk. Damien kept his distance from her, allowing her to lead the way in silence. It wasn't long before she turned to face him with concern about her features.

"What happened to your parents?"

Damien squinted at her, looking around before landing on her again. "Very interesting topic of conversation. What made you choose it?"

"There is just so much I don't know about you. A lot of things I don't understand."

"Right, my sentiments exactly."

"Maybe...this will get easier if we know each other better."

Damien nods, his lips curving a bit as he tries to fight an oncoming smile. His mischievous eyes glinted even in the dim light, Neveah's breath hitching as he walked past her.

"Follow me, I know a place where we can talk."

Neveah followed behind the tall man warily, her eyes wild as they looked out for any source of danger. She wasn't sure why she was so on edge. She held herself in hopes of comfort, her anxiety getting the best of her as her heartbeat increased. She had suddenly stopped upon entering a secret walkway within the hedge. Damien continued without stopping, forcing Neveah to rush forward until the hedge opened. Before her, a vast and beautiful secluded area of the garden. There was a single octagon shaped gazebo which harbored two chairs and a small table inside the confides of its gold ornate structure. The sight contrasted greatly against the midnight sky. Damien continued his walk forward as Neveah slowly followed. He entered the gazebo; amusement clear on his features as he motioned her to sit in one of the large chairs. She did so carefully, her eyes tearing apart her new surroundings like a hawk. Damien sat opposite her, kicking his leg up and over his knee as he sat back with a deep sigh.

"I come here all the time. It's a quiet place, peaceful."

"It's very nice."

"My mother had this constructed." He stated, his brows furrowing as he recalled Medici telling him about it.

"I see why. I could stay out here forever. It's so quiet."

Damien watched her as she finally seemed to relax, closing her eyes for a moment before she opened them to meet his dark green gaze.

"Do you have siblings?" he asked curiously.

"No, unfortunately. I always wanted them though."

Damien scoffed in amusement.

"You can have mine."

Neveah allowed herself to chuckle, her hand immediately going to shield her smile as she looked down to avoid his gaze. Damien cleared his throat, sitting forward in his seat before speaking.

"Do you prefer solitude? Rather than be around others?" Damien inquired carefully, Neveah blinking a few times as she registered his question.

"I do, I prefer being alone. I mean…it's always been that way. I'm most comfortable when I'm by myself."

"I too prefer time to myself, though I have been finding it hard as of late. It's an odd feeling, I can't quite place it. It's very new."

Neveah's head tilted. "Now that I think of it, me too. It feels…empty but there's an ache. Almost like a longing."

Damien's eyes lit up, his body moving forward in his chair a bit.

"That's the perfect description of it. You're good with words."

"Thanks, I enjoy reading—"

"—me too. Do you have a favorite book?"

"That's a hard question, I've read so many."

"If you had to choose at this moment, which would it be?"

Neveah pondered her response, a little war going on within herself as she tried to reach a perfect answer.

"I had read one from the Earth realm. *To Kill a Mockingbird.*"

"Is that so?"

"You sound surprised."

"No, I thought you would have chosen something more...f eminine."

"So, you're undermining my femininity based on my choice of book?"

"That's not what I'm saying...I truly don't even know what I'm saying..."

"Do you have a favorite book?" She asked, trying to change the course of the conversation.

"I recently read a playwright by Edmond Rostand called *Cyrano de Bergerac.* I enjoyed it."

Neveah smiled at his answer, the conversation seeming to flow in a positive direction again.

"I have yet to read it."

"Whenever you'd like to, you can. It's in my study with the rest of my collection."

Damien stops himself, not wanting to bore her with book conversation. He tries and ultimately fails to change the topic in a more exciting direction.

"What is your favorite color?

Neveah laughs genuinely now, her smile reaching her eyes as she tries her best to stop. She didn't want to make him feel bad, but the question felt so random and juvenile. She couldn't help but be amused.

"What?" Damien asks, confusion apparent in his question as she shook her head in reassurance.

"Nothing, it's just a very random question. My favorite color...light blue; like the sky…" she said, closing her eyes briefly as if she was reminiscing on a special moment.

Damien nodded, the silence between them bubbling over as Damien scrunched his brows.

"Mine is green." He stated lowly, almost to himself, trying to find some commonality in sharing his choice.

"I know." Neveah responded nonchalantly, only to have him be completely caught off guard by her answer.

"You know?" He mocked; Neveah nodded.

"Mhm."

"How would you know that?"

"The dress. The one I wore to dinner the first evening I was here. It was the first time you ever complimented me, and it was because of the color of the dress. You also wear emerald cufflinks every day. It was honestly just a lucky guess."

He blinked slowly, allowing a full smile to creep onto his hauntingly handsome face. "You're also very observant." He stated, adding onto his previous statement regarding her intelligence.

"Listen, I don't mean to pry, but…" Nevaeh looks at the man before her warily, wondering if what she was about to ask next was a mistake. "I really want to know about you. Your life…how it was like growing up here. Your parents? Did you ever go to school? Everything else is superficial, to me at least. Yeah, your likes and dislikes make you who you are now but…what shaped those choices? Am I making any sense?" Neveah says, trying to laugh lightly to not seem overbearing.

Damien only stared at her; his green eyes boring into her brown ones as he savored the tension between them. He liked the idea of her being so curious about him, yet a part of him knew it was so wrong of her to be. Dangerous, more like it. He shifted in his seat, blinking hard a few times before he scrunched his brows in thought. Every time he thought he would answer, he stopped himself. What could he say to that loaded question? It was the first time he had been rendered speechless by the angel, a moment he would save forever in his mind.

"I would like to hear your theory first, if that's an acceptable answer."

It was Neveah's turn to be dumbfounded, as she expected him to dodge her attempt like before or become angry at her continued curiosity. She felt her cheeks warm, a slight tinge of pink covering them as she felt herself go blank. She didn't want to offend him; I mean he is the King of Hell. What if he banished her or punished her for her oncoming statements?

"Your mother…she was a kind soul. She made sure you were always taken care of. It seems that way, anyway. You're always very well put together, so tactful—even when you speak."

Damien hummed, acknowledging Neveah's statement as she continued.

"As for your father…I presume he was a strict kind of man. Very serious, very to the point. A part of me even thinks he was hard on you. You are very hard to read; mysterious, closed off, even."

Damien blinks a few times, sitting back in his seat as he angles his arm behind his head. The action took Neveah's focus, seeing him in such a vulnerable yet powerful position. She shook her head slightly and looked away.

"Interesting." Is all he uttered, his jaw jutting slightly as his eyes studied her. "How did you come to those conclusions?"

"I just assumed, based on what I've observed. You did say I was *very* observant."

"How did you know about my mother?"

"Sorry? We all have mothers; I didn't think that would've surprised you."

He chuckled, but it wasn't like before. There was annoyance in the tone, the deep rasp of it even threatening. Neveah's playful smile dropped as he sat forward again, placing his elbows on his knees as he placed his hands together in a praying motion. He closed his eyes and smiled, bringing his joined hands up to his face before slanting them towards her.

"Who told you about my mother?"

Neveah shook her head, her eyes searching his to see if he was joking or being serious. When she noticed his serious features were unwavering, she quickly answered his question.

"I had asked Lennox about her. You wouldn't talk to me, so I wanted to see if someone else knew something—anything about you."

He stared at Neveah for a moment before nodding, a ghost of a smile on his face before it faded completely.

"Right. Lennox." He nearly scoffs, trying his best but failing at hiding his obvious bubbling anger.

"Are you upset?" She asks rhetorically, seeing if he would be honest in the moment.

Damien abruptly stands then without a word, causing her to rush to her feet in a mix of anxiousness and guilt. She asks him again, though this time her words are very pointed, and her delivery is strong.

"Damien, are you upset?"

He looks at her curiously, watching as her face contorts into one of concern at his silence.

"I'm not." He lies bitterly, his clenched jaw clearly giving him away.

"Please, don't punish him. It was my fault for prying, I kept pushing him to talk. If you should be upset at anyone it should be me." She stated, feeling his anger, and knowing what he could do with it.

Damien nods in reply, walking down the path towards the entrance of the garden as Neveah stood in place. She wanted to reach out and talk to him more, though she didn't want to keep pushing him. She could clearly tell he was upset, even sad at the mention of his mother. She looked down, before taking her seat again in defeat.

"I'm sorry." She whispered into the hot air, a silent apology to the man she desperately wanted to know. It was almost like she was apologizing to the light rustling of the hedge leaves around her, her hands claiming her face in a mix of embarrassment and sadness.

It was approaching footsteps which caused her to look up quickly, trying her best to compose herself again only to fall apart once she saw who it was. Damien walked back towards her; his brows scrunched in pure frustration as he stopped a few feet from where the angel sat bewildered. The two stared at each other for a moment as Damien seemed to struggle to find the right words to say.

"My mother died giving birth to me."

Neveah was stunned in silence. It was like she felt a ton of bricks fall onto her chest because of how heavy it suddenly felt. Tears pricked her eyes as she watched Damien standalone before her. He probably has never said that out loud, let alone confess that to another soul. It was such a loaded statement; she couldn't help the tears that finally fell from her eyes.

"I didn't even get to meet her. I've only seen her through pictures. I only know her through stories of what others have told me. Do you know how that feels?"

Neveah stands then, as she slowly makes her way over to him. Damien was visibly trembling, be it from anger or sadness, Neveah couldn't tell. She carefully reached for his arm in attempts to calm him down, but he stepped back.

"I was always told how kind she was, how she was always so courteous and good to others…then I came along and killed her— "

"—no—" Neveah interjected strongly, successfully grabbing his hand as she gave it a gentle but reassuring squeeze before he snatched it from her warm grasp.

"—don't say that. You didn't kill her."

"I did, and my father hated me for it. It's why he left. He couldn't stand the sight of me. The one person he loved and would burn cities to the ground for—taken by some kid who shouldn't have even been born to begin with."

Neveah closes her eyes in pain upon hearing his harsh words, trying to find the right words to tell him before she shakes her head.

"I'm not sure why your father left, but I'm sure it wasn't because of you."

"You don't even know. You don't know me; you don't know what life is like here. You don't even know…"

Neveah nodded once, looking up at him now as he tried his hardest to hold back the tears in his eyes. "You're right, I don't. I don't know anything about you or about this realm because I'm not from here but, I was put here for a reason. The reason, well…I'm not too sure of yet. Though I'm trying my best to get to know you and your way of life, but it seems like you aren't interested in letting me do that."

Neveah retreats her grasp from his hand, a dull ache now seeping in Damien's chest at the action. It had felt so natural, so right, when she held onto him. Now he felt cold again, cold, and alone. He despised the feeling once he felt what it could be replaced with.

"Listen— "He began but was quickly cut off by the angel who began to walk away from him.

"—I understand, so you don't have to waste your time explaining yourself to me. I'm an outsider, I have no idea what you've been through."

"Don't pity me." He spits angrily, losing control of his growing frustration as he looks at the equally enraged angel who turned to face him.

"Pity you? I don't pity you, Damien, because you don't have to act this way. You let your environment consume you, and for that I have no room for remorse or pity for you."

She had walked away without another word, her eyes brimming with fresh tears out of pure anger. She felt that she put herself in a vulnerable position by being upfront and honest with him, but he was just too closed off for any intimate conversation. She had understood why he probably felt this way, he barely knew her. Why would he mouth off about his childhood traumas and scorned life to a stranger? It was a heavy topic of discussion, one that left her upset in the end.

She had retreated to her room, allowing herself to feel the sadness she had tried so hard to hold back on her journey there. She sat upon her bed, groaning as tears fell from her eyes. Neveah felt stupid for being so…open. She was foolish to think The King of Hell would be so cool with sharing his intimate life details. She tried to push past what happened but kept feeling that heavy pang in her chest. She was mortified and angry at herself for thinking so much of an interaction. She laid upon the black velvet bed duvet of the large bed, her eyes dancing upon the detailed artwork that adorned the ceiling. Fire, blood, death, demons…she closed her eyes then, controlling her breathing before turning on her side. She was confused, at war with herself. Why would she want to stay in such a retched place? She kept asking herself the same question. Then it had dawned on her—maybe it was meant to be. Nevaeh always believed in fate, and she had jumped off that cliff holding fate so close to her heart. So, why would she be so abrasive in her wake? She had made a conscious decision to try. Try to acclimate, try to make this work. Though, she felt that every time she tried to make an impression, it fell apart immediately. She sat up then, holding onto herself as she looked about the room, her eyes settling upon the small couch that sat beneath the large window across the room. Her mind drifted to Damien, as she imagined him standing before her sitting frame with his hands in his pockets. The stern but curious glint in his eyes always got her, she couldn't help the increase of her heart at the thought of him looking at her. She sighed, shaking her head slightly before standing to her feet.

Just as she was about to settle in for the night, a knock sounded at the door. She froze in place, her head slowly turning to the closed door as she could hear her heavy breathing in the otherwise silence of the large room. She knew who it was; she could feel the anxiousness—*his* anxiousness. She had taken solace in it, a small smile crossing her features as she slowly made her way to the door. She had placed her hand over the door, her palm flush against the cool gold details as she leaned her forehead on the door. With a shaky breath, she prepared herself for what would come next. She then turned the knob and opened her bedroom door.

CHAPTER 13

THE BLACK BALL

"I'm afraid you have no choice, lovely. It's tradition." Lennox says as he looks at Neveah, who is quite overwhelmed. Her black lace gown contrasted beautifully against her olive toned skin, her chest rose and fell a bit dramatically as she tried to prepare herself for the upcoming evening.

"I can't breathe." She confessed breathlessly, Lennox scoffing at her dramatics.

"Oh, stop it, you have a body, and you need to show it off. Did you really think I was going to squander the opportunity to put you in a corset? You're clearly mistaken. I'm bloody tired of seeing you walking around looking like a box in those god-awful silk slips that are three times too big for you."

A stifled chuckle slipped past Nova's lips, her eyes meeting Nevaeh's wide ones before she cleared her throat and averted her eyes to the lace of Nevaeh's waistline.

Neveah groans, rolling her eyes. "I like to be comfortable and I'm not the begging-for-attention type."

"Oh, get real. You're an Angel in Hell, might as well walk around with a blinding marque that says, *look at me!*"

Neveah tries her best not to laugh at his joke, though her laugh comes out in huffs as she fails to keep serious. Lennox pressed his lips together to keep from chuckling before a round of knocks at the door prompted them to quiet. Lennox instructed Nova to answer it, Nevaeh's breath hitching once she saw the grandiose doors to Lennox's studio open with a gust of warm air. The royal guard began lining up on either side of the doorway promptly as Davina and Medici were the first two to enter, casually dressed in very macabre yet sublime attire.

"Neveah, you look stunning. That color suits you so well." Davina almost gawks, her hands clasping together as she admires the angel in black. Medici nods in agreement.

"She's right, you do look marvelous. Damien will be pleased."

Davina elbows him and gives him a knowing look, causing him to look at her in confusion.

Neveah clears her throat, smoothing her bodice as she spoke, "Thank you, though it feels wrong— "

"—feels wrong yet looks completely right, quite fitting for your situation, yes?" Damien's deep voice booms as he walks into the room, causing every hair on Neveah's body to stand up right. Again, she was rendered speechless by his presence, something she realized happened very often when he was around.

He looked daunting yet so classy, his usual black on black attire felt a bit different this time around. She looked him over, studying his frame as he drew nearer. Her eyes immediately landed on his wrists. The area which would usually harbor his emerald, green cufflinks were now substituted with light blue opal gems. Her jaw fell slack at the sight, knowing how personal the subtle change must have been for him. Also, how he had remembered that fine detail when she shared her favorite color. Was that intentional? She had pushed the thought aside as he finally stopped in front of her. She could smell a heady mix of smoke and sandalwood, and the subtle lingering smell of bourbon.

"Hi." He greeted lowly once he stood in front of her, his eyes greedily raking over her form as she tried to calm her racing heart.

"Hi." she responded, her voice coming out in a short breath as they stared at once another in silence, Nova and Lennox moving quickly around her as they provided finishing touches to her gown and hair.

Medici and Davina looked on in a mix of dismay and anticipation. Their mouths were slightly open in surprise at the small, courteous, yet very flirtatious interaction between Damien and Nevaeh. Their eyes followed Damien as he slowly reached upward towards Neveah's face, brushing a curl from her line of sight before tracing his fingers down and along her exposed collar bone. Davina's eyes popped out of her head, her jaw nearly hitting the floor as Medici cleared his throat loudly. He nudged

Davina expectedly, his eyes stern as he non-verbally told her to stop with her childish reactions.

"You'll catch flies if you keep it up, Dav." Damien stated rather coolly, his eyes casually moving to meet her wide ones with a smug grin.

"Oh, shut up, dickhead." She spat in embarrassment, groaning as she prompted Medici and Lennox to follow her to the event with a round of snaps and crazed motioning towards the exit.

Nevaeh kept her gaze cast down, feeling the flush of her cheeks on full display as Damien moved towards Lennox's worktable, lightly tracing his fingers over the many fabrics which covered the area. Nova nodded her head slightly at Nevaeh, her eyes cast downward, and she twisted her hands together.

"May I get you anything else, Lady Nevaeh?"

The angel shook her head briskly, offering a small smile toward the timid seamstress.

"Not at this moment, Nova. Thank you for all your help."

Nova nodded once more before turning and walking out of the studio, leaving Damien and Nevaeh alone in the room.

"All his hard work paid off; I see."

Neveah tried to keep her cool, smoothing over her bodice again as she allowed a low shaky breath to release past her lips upon hearing him.

"Yes, Lennox is very passionate about what he does. Only if it exceeds your expectations, though, is the only way Lennox is content with his work."

"I'm very pleased." He responds lowly, his eyes immediately locking with hers before he takes his time walking up to her with his hands behind his back.

"You do look exceptional this evening, Neveah. Black is truly your color."

"Sure, it is." She replied sarcastically, her eyes widening slightly in a mix of embarrassment and surprise. She meant to speak to herself in her head, a bit of inflated ego the only thing able to get her through this anxiety filled scenario.

"Oh? Well, if you'd excuse my lack of knowledge. I do have a lot on my plate, you know, being King and all."

"What's it to you anyway?" Neveah playfully countered, looking up through her lashes at the dashing man before her as she tried to make the conversation more lighthearted. "I'm pretty sure you've seen a bunch of women in luxurious black attire. I'm just like all the rest."

He hangs his head to the side, a sly smirk marking his structured face. "All the rest? I'm not too sure about that."

"Why would that be?" She asks, still playful yet her question held a curios edge.

"The difference between you and every other woman I cross paths with is, I don't find myself wondering what colors they look good in or how they look without any clothes at all. I'm well rounded in that regard."

Neveah's face twists then, a clear look of distaste on full display as Damien's eyes turn playful.

"Does that bother you?"

"What?"

"Your face, it said everything your mouth didn't."

"Yeah, well that's just how I am."

"So, you're jealous?"

"How did you end up at that conclusion?"

"You didn't even let me finish my spiel before you cursed me out with your face."

Neveah looked away from him, crossing her arms as she held her stance. "I really don't care about what you think anyway, because like I said, and based on what you just said, you're used to being around elegantly dressed women who you compliment persistently in attempts to make their hearts race and quite possibly end up doing sinful acts with in private. Me? You won't snare me up in your little game. I'm ten steps ahead of you, sir. I won't give in to your little shenanigans. I'm too smart for that."

Damien watches her in a mix of what seems like admiration and amusement. "Fine. Since you've already made up your mind, I'll refrain from trying to 'ensnare' you in my sinful agenda. Though, I'm glad you've figured me all out in just a months' time; that's record breaking. So, what I'll say next won't affect you at all, right, since you're so 'self-aware' of the situation?"

Neveah turns her head to look at him now, his unwavering stare making her heart jump just a bit. She cocks her head and brow, almost challenging him. He carefully sweeps his slender digits over her bare collarbone once more, allowing his touch to raise goosebumps over her soft skin. He watches the action with pristine focus, moving down the length of her bare arm before his eyes flickered up to hers. She resembled a deer in headlights, the picture causing Damien to crack a smile as he cocked his brow.

"You're very different from other women I've encountered simply because you don't think like them, you don't have the same values, or morals. You haven't thrown yourself at me once. It's quite refreshing, really. So, seeing you dressed up on my account excites me more than you know. Now imagine…"

Neveah's breath hitched as he careened his hand to her lower back, pulling her closer as she then placed her hand out to create an inch of distance. A devilish grin crossed Damien's features, leaning forward just a bit to tease her even more.

"…imagine how I feel just thinking of how you'd look in a said 'sinful' encounter with me."

A deep blush washed over the angel's face, her arms immediately breaking free of his embrace as she lowly gasped in surprise. She pushed past Damien, attempting to walk past him in sheer embarrassment before he grabbed her wrist to keep her from running. He pulled her close again, this time their bodies were pressed against one another with no room between their chests. Damien's eyes were almost lustful in appearance, his devilish but smug grin on full display. Neveah pressed her forehead against his chest in attempts to shield him from her deep red face.

"I bet you've never had anyone talk about you like that, hm?"

"How about you just be quiet?" She retorted, her voice coming out strained as she couldn't think of a better comeback.

"Surely, angel."

Damien found himself overwhelmed by the number of people he had to entertain at the annual Black Ball. He was more than halfway through his introduction when Davina stepped in to save him.

"Excuse me, may I steal The King? It's important."

The man raised his glass with a small smile, nodding in agreement as Damien and Davina casually walked from the guest.

"I would thank you, but you'd hold it over my head in the future, so I'll refrain." Damien huffs, sipping his dark liquor as Davina rolled her eyes.

"Whatever. What you need to do is go handle your royal pain in the ass, who, by the way, is hiding from me. I mean, really? She's like a little kid. Little does she know; though, she sucks at hiding but I'm not going to be the one to tell her that."

"Where is she?" He asks smoothly, tipping his glass to easily down the rest of the poignant liquor in his stout glass.

"Library." She blatantly responds, nearly snatching his empty glass before they glare at one another in annoyance.

"Try not to be so overbearing and scare off the guests—" Damien teases.

"—choke and die." She seethes, pushing past a smug Damien as he casually makes his way through the crowd and towards the west wing to the library.

Neveah sat comfortably on the ground, her beautiful gown splayed in every direction as she carefully picked up an assortment of books and flipped through them. She was so excited to have found this place on her way back from the restroom, deciding this would be a better use of her time than being anxious in a room filled with the entirety of its realm's population.

Her dark brown eyes greedily scanned the assortment of titles in front of her, a small smile placing itself on her face as she flipped through the pages of a book about Earth. She gripped the semi-worn book as she stood again, practically floating through the moonlit room with grace. She lightly traced the bindings of the books as she walked through the aisles, her eyes scanning the titles before she stopped. She quickly reaches forward and grabs a book, her brows furrowed in surprise at the title. Just one word, almost brandished into the middle center of the cover.

Heaven. Her nimble fingers were quick to grab the book from its snug position on the shelf, before opening it just as fast. Her eyes tried to adjust to the low light of the room in attempts to read the first passage before she jumped at the sound of the library doors opening. She quickly closed the book, clutching the closed text to her chest as she turned to conceal herself behind an adjacent bookshelf.

Damien entered casually, already sensing her bubbling anxiety as he slowly walked into the center of the room. He placed his hands in his pockets, looking forward and out of the top to bottom window that allowed the moon to illuminate the otherwise dark space. He carefully removed his suit jacket, walking over to place it over one of the few chairs surrounding him. He sighed, loosening the top of his black tie. Neveah was mesmerized at the sight, her heart beating at an obscene rate. She felt like she was spying on him. Did he come here to get away too?

"You know, it would be easier if you came out on your own. It would save me the energy, as I'm not really in the mood to play hide-and-seek."

Neveah paled, her back hitting the shelf behind her as she tried to remain still. Damien's eyes flickered up to the second floor of the room, a smirk clear on his face as he knew her location now. Neveah let a small shaky breath leave her lips as she turned and walked up the aisle to the marble railing. She stopped with conviction, looking over the railing and at Damien, who looked astonishing bathed in the moonlight. The two stared at one another for a moment, almost relishing the sight of one another before he broke the silence.

"So, were you just going to stay here the entire night?"

Her mouth opened to speak but nothing came out, so she shook her head as she tried to quickly think of a smart comeback.

"Absolutely not. I just got distracted."

"Distracted?" he presses.

"That is what I said."

Damien allowed a small chuckle to reverberate in the moonlit room, his hands working along his collar as he adjusted the lining.

"If you're scared you can tell me."

"Scared? What would I be afraid of?" She replied quickly, her brows furrowing as she tried not to be defensive.

"Well, you tell me. You're the one hiding behind a bookshelf in my library when you should be in the main hall mingling with the elites."

"I wasn't hiding before; I only did when you entered. Plus, I have no place in the main hall with your people. What am I going to discuss with them, hm? The second coming of Christ? Oh, I'm sure they'll love that."

"So, what? You're scared of me, then?"

"I never said that, stop twisting my words around. I didn't know it was you at first when you came in."

Damien tilted his head, watching her as she avoided his eyes.

"Come down here." He said deeply, motioning in front of him as Neveah pushed herself against the railing.

"No, thank you."

He looked up at her through his lashes, then down to the floor before letting his head fall back in mock defeat.

"Don't make me chase you."

"I thought that's what you were already doing."

The silence that ensued was deafening, Damien's jaw fell slack at her statement as Neveah's eyes widened in shock. She had a real knack for speaking out loud when she didn't really want to. His eyes seemed to deepen, his features suddenly darkening as he gripped the back of a chair and dragged it out to the middle of the room where he stood previously. He sat down slowly, his eyes never leaving hers as he spread his legs out in front of him before crossing his right ankle over his left knee. She looked away, feeling embarrassed at his almost intrusive stare as he cleared his throat.

"Let's get one thing straight, angel. I don't chase, I attract. Though, if I do want something, I get it. It doesn't matter what it is."

"Sounds like something a narcissist would say."

"Am I a narcissist?"

"I'm still figuring you out."

He nods, seeming to let her words sink in.

"I also am not a fan of others disobeying me."

"I guess we won't be getting along well then."

"Oh, no, we will...because I know how to handle insubordination."

"Is that so?"

"For sure."

"How do you handle it, my lord and savior?" she mockingly asked, her tone patronizing as she rolled her eyes.

She began to slowly make her way towards the stairs which she began to descend.

"It's not so much of saying how, I just do it. I'm more of a hands-on kind of teacher."

Neveah could sense his underlying inappropriate connotation, her hands shaking slightly as she made it to the ground floor. She tried to remain unfazed by his cryptic words. Confident, even.

"Why did you even come here? You should be entertaining your guests."

"Yeah, and?"

"You're the King…" she stated matter-of-factly, motioning with her hands to almost get him thinking.

"That's right, sweetheart."

"Don't call me that!" She nearly spat as he put his hands up with a playful smirk.

"My, my, angel. So much fire in that innocent little body. No wonder why they let you out scott-free."

"You don't know what you're talking about!" She rushed forward, her bubbling frustration leaving her right where he wanted her.

She stood right in front of him, his smug demeanor angering her further as she crossed her arms.

"Look at you," he began lightheartedly, his voice then dropping a bit in tone as he stood tall before her from his once seated position. It caught her off guard, as she had forgotten that he almost towered over her in height.

"I told you that I never chased, you came right to me." He replied smugly, her hand winding back as she had attempted to smack him.

He caught her wrist before she could strike, his eyes wild as the two stared at one another.

"I am not one of your toys, and I certainly won't be one of your slaves that obey everything you say."

Damien allowed her wrist to fall from his grasp, stepping away from her for a moment before going to retrieve his jacket. He motions for her to follow him out of the library.

"If you're going to flake at an event at least do it on my account."

"Thank you so much for coming, it was a pleasure to see you." Davina spoke rather sweetly, shaking the hands of some of the high-status members as they made their way out of the castle.

"I must say, King Damien seemed rather preoccupied with this visit. I'm sure with good reason?" One of them asked, curiosity settling in his tone as Davina did her best to remain unfazed.

"My deepest apologies on behalf of the King, he has been very busy as of late. His hands have been full but, I promise you he will have your undivided attention at the Blood Ball."

The man nods, his eyes stern as he shakes Davina's hand strongly.

"I will be looking forward to it. Although the Blood Ball is more of an informal and vivacious gathering, we will be making up for the lost time of tonight."

"Absolutely. You get back safely."

After an hour of apologizing to guests of Damien's blatant absence, Davina nearly collapsed on the stairs in a mix of annoyance and tiredness. Dante watched her from the end of the hall, admiring her obvious sleepy features as she removed her abstract heels. His admiration was cut short upon Medici's entrance, his voice booming through the otherwise empty hall.

"It's finally over. I despise the Black Ball with everything in me, I am always so elated when we close the doors late at night. I could just jump with joy." He says, his voice jovial as he clapped his hands together.

"I wish I harbored your same enthusiasm. Kind of burnt out from covering Damien's ass, for the billionth time."

Medici's smile faded, clearing his throat as he sighed in realization.

"He skipped halfway through, didn't he?"

"Yeah, he did. Though he wasn't the only culprit."

Medici then looked over to Dante, who stood tall.

"Do you know where he is?" He asked nonchalantly, Davina standing as she crossed her arms.

"Yeah." Dante confessed childishly, looking down at his boots as Davina scoffed.

"I'm going to sleep. I'm tired of this."

Davina's body disappeared past Dante as she left to settle in for the night, leading Medici to slowly walk towards him.

"Don't worry about her, she's had too much social interaction for one night."

Dante chuckles, nodding in understanding as he sighs.

"I'm going to need a favor from you, for the Blood Ball. Take a walk with me?"

"You're afraid, just say it." Damien scoffed in amusement, his smirk on full display as Neveah shook her head.

"I am not afraid, I am just not interested, okay?" She nearly spits back in defiance, her eyes dancing from the liquor filled glass to Damien's playful eyes.

"I know you're afraid."

"You don't know me enough to say that."

"No, I most definitely do. I know you well enough."

"I've had that putrid drink before. Maybe if you paid attention a bit more you would know that."

"You've never had this before, Neveah." He states matter-of-factly.

"Yeah, I have, Damien. When I first landed in his hellish place. I was offered it by one of your little kitchen demons. I nearly choked and died because you don't offer water."

"That was a mixer. It barely had alcohol in it."

"Davina was drunk off her ass with it, so, I don't know what you're talking about."

"Davina drinks onyx spiritus straight. She wasn't drinking what you had."

"I'm not drinking that!" She exclaims, her hands pointing to the tall glass with the bubbling red liquor.

"You're missing out," He begins, his voice adopting a deeper tone.

"...how do you know if you don't like it if you've never even tried it?"

Neveah looks up at him, his dark eyes piercing hers over his glass as she almost shakes with frustration.

"I guess I'll never know."

"That's too bad. Well, how about this,"

He places his glass down and stretches his arms out a bit, tilting his head a bit resulting in a slight crack. He levels his shoulders, placing his hands on his slanted leg.

"Every sip of that drink equals a question you can ask me—and I'll have to answer it."

Her eyes widened then, her gaze settling upon the bubbling drink before carefully reaching out to grasp it. She tried to hide her slight embarrassment for taking the bait so quickly. Damien gauged her reaction, a smirk taking its place on his face as he sat back. He motioned for her to continue; amusement still very apparent in his gaudy features as Neveah clutched the glass with all her might.

"This is blackmail at this finest."

"Drink up, won't you, angel?"

Neveah carefully brings the glass up to her lips, taking the tiniest sip possible before coughing.

"You're so dramatic." Damien scoffs playfully, rolling his eyes as he grabs his drink again, taking a decent sip from it.

Neveah shudders outwardly, her face twisting in disgust as she shook her head once. Damien watched her casually, a bit of anticipation bubbling at the idea of her asking him questions. She was always filled with surprises; he didn't know what to expect.

"Okay…question number one,"

Damien nods his head in agreement, a small smile crossing his lips before it is gone entirely.

"…How old were you when you became King?"

"I give you an ultimatum, and that's the question you ask me?"

"I'll be asking you a lot more."

"Oh, really? Should I call for another bottle?" Damien asks heartily, his eyes almost lighting up at the back and forth going between them.

Neveah ignores him, closing her eyes briefly before continuing.

"Age?"

"Sixteen."

"Really? That's young to rule an entire realm."

"I had guidance. Medici's like my own guardian Angel," he chuckles, his glass lowering from his lips before looking at her.

"Well, besides you, now."

They stare at one another for a moment before Neveah almost snatches the glass with alcohol, taking another sip. She braces herself for the pungent taste, the intense burning sensation as it settles in her chest. She shakes her head again, still not used to the taste and its aftereffects.

"What happened to your father?"

Damien blinks slowly, carefully swirling the almost finished red liquor in his stout glass before sighing heavily. He seemed to hesitate, but he answered her anyway. He leaned forward and placed his glass on the table before them.

"He left when I took the throne."

"What do you mean by left?"

"Is that another question?"

Neveah groaned, grabbing hold of her glass in frustration as Damien held his hand up to halt her actions. His lips curved upward in amusement as he slowly answered her question. He realized how quick she was to listen to him, her anxiousness bubbling over.

"He abandoned me and the realm. He hated me to begin with, so it was easier to go when the transfer of power happened."

"So, where did he go? I mean, he's Satan."

"Earth, where you so desperately want to go."

Neveah pondered his statement as he poured her more liquor and then himself.

"Do you know what he's doing? I mean…have you ever tried looking for him?"

"No reason to."

Neveah shut her mouth then, her lips forming a straight line as she didn't want to press him on matters which made him angry or uncomfortable. She could tell the topic was sensitive, even for someone who is supposedly cold hearted and insensitive to others' own feelings. She lifted the glass to her lips, drinking before immediately asking a question.

"How old are you?"

His gaze darkened a little, a bit of playfulness in his eyes as he watched her face twist.

"How old do you think I am?"

"You said you'd answer my questions."

"I am."

"You're playing around, why not just answer it. What, are you like, an old man?"

Damien chuckles genuinely then, smoothing his face as he raises his glass towards her.

"Leave it to you to keep me grounded, thank you."

Her eyes widen as she cranes her neck out a bit, signaling her growing impatience.

"Twenty-nine."

Neveah's face relaxes then, not expecting such a normal answer from someone like him.

"Did you expect me to be old and omnipotent?"

"No, you look…I just—I had imagined you could take the form of whatever you wanted but be much older. I thought you'd be much scarier looking."

"Is that what they taught you upstairs?"

"You don't like Heaven all that much, do you?"

"What makes you say that?"

Neveah sighs, relaxing her shoulders as she looks out at the dark sky.

"You always make little indirect statements, like you're making fun of it."

"Yeah, because I am."

Neveah scowls at his nonchalant manner, as he finds it the most amusing thing ever.

"You don't know much about Heaven, Damien. Look where you were raised. There are so many great things Heaven has to offer. For example," she begins, her voice taking a tone of excitement as she places her hands together in thought. Before she could continue, Damien interjected, his hand shooting outwards to halt her.

"Sorry, I'm agnostic."

She gives him a look, before a small smile placed itself on her dainty features.

"Very funny. Though you should really think about everything you don't know about Heaven before making assumptions and mocking it. I think you'll be more understanding of how I feel once you really know what it's like."

"Sounds like you should reap what you sow, Angel."

She nods once, looking down at her hands in her lap upon realizing what he said.

"You're right, I apologize if I've been rude. It was never my intention."

"Cheers," he says suddenly, raising his glass up,

"—to us finally becoming self-aware."

Neveah nods, a smile on her lips as she carefully clanked her glass with his before taking another sip.

"Why did you sit beside my bed all that time? You know when I got hurt?"

Damien stood quietly for a moment, trying his best to put into words what it was like.

"It was a very interesting experience for me. I've never felt like that before, for anyone. Yeah, I've gotten a bit nervous when Davina got sick or even Medici but…I always knew they'd be alright. With you, I couldn't tell."

"Were you afraid?"

"Afraid?" he asks, his brows tugging together as his tone sounded almost defensive.

"Yes. Were you afraid of what might happen to me?"

"I'm not sure what the feeling was. At times I felt afraid, sure. Other times I felt anxious, sometimes even defeated. Then there was this— "he placed his hand on his chest, his gaze focused on the table.

"—this aching. It was like my heart was hurting if that makes sense."

"It does. I know that feeling."

Damien nodded once, drinking in response as Neveah continued.

"Have you ever been in love with anyone— "she asked carefully, though it seemed to catch Damien off guard.

He had scrunched his brows, his face contorting into a mix of confusion and bewilderment at the sudden and loaded question.

"—or not, sorry, am I making you uncomfortable?"

"No, but that's a deep question to ask out of the blue."

"Let's just move on— "

"—no, I…I thought I was once. Though I've come to realize I wasn't in love. Just lustful."

"I've never heard of that before."

He cocks his brow, before answering,

"You're in the right place, then. You'll know all about it soon enough."

"So, you were infatuated with this person?"

"No, it was the other way around. Morana is still heavily in love with me and does her best to crawl back into my life."

"Morana…how long have you known her?"

"Since I was a child. We were close growing up, it turned romantic just before I became King."

"What happened to her? Did she…" Neveah asks, insinuating the worst which only causes Damien to laugh.

"Oh, I wish. She's alive, I'm afraid. You'll meet her at the Blood Ball. She never misses a good party." He downs the last of his liquor as Neveah nods in understanding.

"Should I be worried?" She utters, causing Damien to sigh.

"She'll probably try to make you cry, but you shouldn't worry about Morana. I'll take care of her."

Damien stands then, adjusting his sleeves before looking down at Neveah.

"Are you happy with my responses this evening?"

Neveah stands, smoothing out her dress.

"I wish we could stay longer. I have so many more questions."

"Walk with me." Damien quipped, beginning his walk out of the garden with Neveah hot on his heels.

"Your guards…excluding Dante, they don't show their face. Why is that?" Neveah asks curiously, tripping over herself briefly before recovering beside him.

He slows his pace, resting his hands behind his back as he continues forward with Neveah now following in his steps.

"They're damned souls, only meant to serve me and nothing else. They're programmed to take orders. What they look like makes no difference to me or anyone else."

Neveah scrunched her brows, crossing her arms over her chest.

"So…do they have faces?"

Damien looked over at her, his grin fighting to take place on his face as he raised his brow.

"Do you think they have faces?"

"I think I asked a serious question."

"Yes, they do. Some are disfigured though, just how they showed up when they entered the realm. Concealing their faces just covers up their blank expression. Also adds a bit of stealth, maybe even instill fear when they battle. They look like creatures more than anything, don't they?"

"You make it sound so whimsical, Damien. It's fucking terrifying."

He stops mid step, turning to her with a wild look in his eyes. Neveah stops too, turning and looking around in a mix of surprise and bubbling fear.

"What? What happened?" she quickly asked, her eyes crazed as she was preparing for the worst in the dim lit aisle of the garden hedge.

"You just cursed, you know that, right?"

Neveah's eyes widened immensely then, her fingers grazing her lips as she covered her mouth in realization.

"I did, didn't I? I am so sorry; I don't know what came over me I— "

"—it felt liberating, didn't it? It just gives a certain edge when expressing your emotions."

"You aren't upset?" She asks genuinely, her voice no more than a whisper as Damien suddenly felt uncomfortable at her embarrassment.

He immediately disliked the feeling, realizing how out-of-place the action was for her.

"Why would I be? It's natural to curse."

"It's a sin."

"Well, you fucking sinned. There is nothing wrong with that. I'm not going to burn you on a stake for it or damn you to

Hell—you're already here." He added comically as he snickered at his comment.

Neveah seemed to relax a bit then, her eyes looking down to the glossy black walkway under their feet.

"You know, I sinned in a big way today…if that makes you feel any better."

"How so?" Neveah asked, the two falling back into their slow-paced walk toward the castle.

"I left the Black Ball. I had a lot of important people here and I abandoned them, though I had a good reason to."

"What was that?" Neveah countered smoothly, her eyes forward as her heart suddenly began to race.

Damien tried to hide his smile as he spoke.

"Just some introverted angel. Had to make sure she wasn't trying to burn the castle to the ground."

Neveah chuckles then, the two finally making their way to the stairs as they ascend them slowly. Neither of them wanted to part from one another or their game of questions, but Damien had to answer for his absence in the evening and Neveah had to prepare herself for her own chastity. The pair finally made it to the castle grounds, turning to one another in silence as they thought of something to say.

"You know, you aren't so scary after all. You had me fooled for a second in the library but, I guess I really shouldn't judge a book based solely on its cover." Neveah confessed, looking up into his eyes as he hung his head low.

"Safe to say, I can agree. Though, you're mine next time—" he stated, lingering closer to her face as Nevaeh suddenly felt the liquor hit her senses like a ton of bricks. She felt intoxicated with him being so close, like he was aiding her airy feeling. She desperately wanted to hold onto it, she secretly wanted to see where this newfound feeling would take her—where it would take them.

"…and I won't be asking such juvenile questions, either."

Damien took a leap, lightly tracing her lips with the tips of his fingers as he suddenly broadened the space between them. Nevaeh breathed deeply in defeat, her eyes glossy and heavy with the mix of intoxication and anticipation.

"Goodnight." He states clearly, turning and walking from a standing Nevaeh who internally turned into gelatin. She opened her mouth to speak, but nothing left past her lips besides a hitched hiccup.

It seemed like an eternity of her standing there in awe, until she slowly turned and began her walk to her room. She couldn't calm the metaphorical butterflies she felt in her stomach, the red bubbling alcohol from before making her feel like she was floating through the grandiose halls. She smiled to herself as she thought about the next time she would see Damien, the image of his deep green eyes etched into her memory for the rest of the night.

CHAPTER 14

REPTILIA

"You're arrogant and self-centered and really fucking annoying, if I hadn't already told you that!" Davina exclaims towards Damien the following morning during their meeting, Damien closing his eyes in defiance as he tries his best not to crack a joke, he knew would send her over the edge.

"I'm sorry, Davina. I was preoccupied." He replied coolly, trying his best to sound genuine as Davina slapped her hand flat on the table.

"I would accept your apology if I knew you weren't being a smartass so—I don't. As for your preoccupation—she will be getting an earful too."

"Davina," Medici interjects, before getting a jagged look from the raven-haired female.

"I was alone the entire banquet and had to answer for his absence. I'm surprised I didn't get swallowed alive by the elites. They were fuming!"

"They'll survive, won't they? They're the same ones who come every year and drink all the booze and smile in my face. They'll be back even if I'm present or not. They can't stand to be without my approval."

"You're really something else, Damien. A fucking prize." She scoffs sarcastically as Damien plays with a toothpick between his teeth in attempts to hide his amusement.

"So, they say, Dav. As for Nevaeh, this isn't her fault, so you'll leave her out of this."

"If I remember correctly, she's the person who kept you from your duties—" Davina stands then, her voice growing louder as Damien sat upright for the first time the entire meeting.

"—if we are discussing memory, it should be you who's to blame for allowing her to leave the party and then telling me to find her. The person who royally fucked up here is none other than you. So, I'd relax before you pop a blood vessel on a matter which really was all your doing."

"You inconsiderate prick! —"

"—THAT'S ENOUGH!" Medici bellowed between the two siblings, standing himself as he looked between the two.

"This bickering must stop. It isn't fixing or changing anything. You two really need to stop this childish back-and-forth."

"I'll stop when he finally grows up and takes responsibility for what he does and acts like the King he's supposed to be."

She spits, causing Damien to scoff as he places his hands in his pockets.

"Maybe I could if you weren't on my back like a leech."

"Out!" Medici exclaimed loudly, motioning for Davina to leave.

She did so with anger, expressing her obvious frustration by kicking her chair back and staring hard at Damien before she walked out without another word. Medici closed his eyes, breathing in heavily before sighing.

"We need to discuss plans moving forward, including Nevaeh."

"What about her?"

"Well, you must marry her. The prophecy says so, and considering order we must abide by it."

"I hardly even know her."

"Hardly? What have you two been doing on your secret rendezvous?"

"I wouldn't call them secret if everyone knows about them."

"It must happen sometime, sooner rather than later. As for her indoctrination into the realm…that's something that will take more time than anything. She has different views, different values—so be patient with her. It will be much easier on you if you do."

Damien sits in his seat again, this time sitting upright as Medici continues.

"Try to teach her about the history of the realm, make her feel a part of it. Oh! Explain to her the mark, as well. I overheard her inquiring about it to poor Lennox. That man is going to catch a heart attack from all the stress one of these days."

"He'll end up back here anyway." Damien mutters, causing Medici to give him a knowing look.

"Also, you must prepare for Morana's arrival as well as the renegade troupe. Though The Blood Ball is months away, this is serious. She will see Nevaeh and things will immediately explode; you know how that woman can be."

"It's handled. Dante is leading security that night. Nevaeh won't leave my sight."

"Are you sure about that? You managed to lose her quite easily the last time."

"Very funny. I'll have everything under control."

"Right. Now, as for Davina— "

"—Davina needs help, as far as I'm concerned. She also needs to check her childish attitude at the door, because I'm getting thin on patience with her."

"Damien, you know she means no harm or disrespect. She is just looking out for you."

"She needs to look out for herself. I don't need anyone's guidance."

Medici nods once, folding his hands in front of him as he looks towards Damien with a small smirk.

"She's being an older sister, remember that the next time she berates you."

"I'm confused, Lennox. I mean when we spend time around one another things flow easily but…"

"…but?" Lennox pries, showing feigned interest in their conversation as he cinches measuring tape around Nevaeh's waist.

"…it's short lived. Sometimes I just feel like I make him uncomfortable with my questions. I don't mean to, it's just that…I'm so curious about who he is and what all this means." She says in an exasperated manner, her hands flinging upward to make her statement more enthusiastic.

Lennox hums in agreement, giving her a reassuring smile as he then turns away from her and to his workstation. His hands roam across the many fabrics and designs, his eyes quickly seeing his sketched design on the paper before him.

"I understand. Though I think you should tell the King about your feelings. Be open and honest."

"I don't know, I don't want to make things harder than they already are."

"It's almost like ripping a band-aid off if you think of it that way. It will probably sting; they'll be fear riddled in the action—was it too soon? Will an infection occur? But, lovely, what you must realize is…wounds need to breathe. They need to be exposed for some time to fully heal. How will you know if you don't take the first step?"

Nevaeh stares at Lennox in a mix of awe and disbelief, her mouth slightly ajar at his perfect metaphor.

"I think, if you're meant to be here from now on—become Queen…you need to establish your relationship and all its components. It will be so relieving for the two of you once that is done."

"When did you become so wise, Lennox?" Nevaeh asked in mock surprise, only causing him to smirk.

"I've been around for a very long time. I used to do all of this for the King once upon a time. Though he got older and therefore more independent. So, I stopped being his hands-on assistant once he inherited the throne. Though before that happened, I was at his side as much as Medici is today."

"Why did you stop being his assistant?"

"Well…it was difficult once his father began pushing him to take the crown. He became frustrated more easily, agitated at the slightest inconvenience. His father didn't approve of me being so available for him. I think he believed I was making him too dependent, weak even. So, once he officially became King, Damien dissolved my position entirely. I spent my days as a council advisor and occasional designer since then, well, that is, until you graced us with your presence."

Nevaeh looks down at her folded hands, unsure of what to say after this pertinent information was shared with her. She almost felt sorry for Lennox. She suddenly felt sad at the thought of devoting her life to being there for someone every day and then just being dismissed without a thought. She closed her eyes briefly as she tried to find her voice again.

"I am so sorry. It sounds like that might have really hurt you when he said he didn't need your help anymore."

Lennox wore a ghost of a smile, almost as if he was reminiscent of his times with Damien all those years ago.

"Well, yes, it did make me sad. Though I realized that he was misinformed from early on and believed he wasn't deserving of any comfort or help. So, once I fully realized that, my sadness was redirected into feelings of remorse. Though that was not very good either. His father was very stern and very strict when it came to young Damien, therefore holding any anger or grudge in my black heart for Damien now would be sorely misplaced."

Nevaeh listened openly and eagerly; in awe of the information, she was receiving. Though it was about Lennox, she felt that she was getting closer to knowing who Damien might really be, or, rather, who he pretends to be.

"I understand. It seems that he had a very demanding upbringing."

"Yes, a very trying time for a child indeed."

Lennox gave a lighthearted chuckle, the sound misplaced among the heavy subject between them as he changed the topic of discussion.

"This gown is going to stop the elites in their tracks. I cannot wait to see their reactions."

"I wish I didn't have to go...it seems like such a pompous event."

"Pompous? Well, it seems that you're a bit biased, aren't you?"

Nevaeh shakes her head defeatedly.

"I just don't belong. I'm going to stick out like a sore thumb,"

"—who said so? You'll stand out for sure, though in the complete opposite way you're thinking."

"Lennox...it just doesn't feel right."

Lennox stops his measurements quickly, looking up at a saddened Nevaeh before claiming her hands in his.

"I know this whole situation has you very confused and you feel at odds with yourself. I promise you, for the centuries I've been alive I can honestly say everything—and I do mean everything—happens for a reason. We all have purpose, though it's with time and tribulations that we find out what that true purpose is. Worry, though you shouldn't let the feeling consume you. Name it, accept it, and then move on. It is the only way you'll truly allow yourself to live a worthy life."

Nevaeh listened, the words touching her deeply as she felt tears slip from her eyes. She carefully reached up and wiped them away, looking at her fingertips in surprise. Lennox claimed her shoulders softly and gave a reassuring squeeze.

"You're crying, why?"

Nevaeh gave a breathy laugh, her lips softly curving upwards into a smile as she continued to stare at her tear-stained finger-tips.

"My father...he used to reassure me like that all the time. I've always been very...uneasy."

Lennox carefully wipes a stray tear from Nevaeh's cheek as he nods in understanding.

"Of course. I am both sorry and glad that I was able to bring back the memory of your father."

"You don't need to apologize; you did nothing wrong. I just hope that he's alright, mother too. I left in such a tragic way, so abrupt…"

Lennox goes back to his worktable a few feet from Nevaeh's standing figure. Her hands find their way together, weaving themselves nervously as she continues to think.

"I can't even imagine how Cassius feels…he must be so hurt."

"Cassius?" Lennox casually asks, his tone curious as Nevaeh pales. She hadn't meant to speak so loudly; she was merely talking lowly to herself in what she thought was the confines of her own mind.

"Yes…Cassius…we were supposed to marry before I left home. I left him at the altar…" She confessed, her brows tugging together as she closed her eyes.

"You were not happy, am I correct in assuming that?" Lennox says, turning around to face her now as she opens her eyes.

"Yes." She managed to say, her voice low and unsteady as she tried to hold back the oncoming tears.

"Then you did the right thing by leaving. No one should live unhappily, especially in marriage."

"What about here, with Damien? I can't leave if I'm not happy with him, Lennox. What then?"

Lennox gives her a knowing look, his eyes holding a certain glint Nevaeh noticed almost immediately.

"I'll bet you that you'll be happier than ever with that one. I would know, I practically raised the hellion."

"What are you wagering?" Neveah said without thinking, causing Lennox to release a piercing laugh that brought a smirk on her lips.

"You're fiery, no wonder you landed here with me, sweetheart."

"Damien always says the same thing." She sheepishly confesses, causing Lennox to hum in knowing agreement.

"Your crown." Lennox states clearly, almost causing Neveah's eyes to pop out of her sockets.

"I'm sorry?"

Lennox rolls his eyes playfully, beginning to remove the many pins from the draped silk and lace attached to her body.

"Your literal crown, I want the statement piece. I want to be able to wear it around and feel like a royal. Deal?" he asks confidently, holding his hand out quickly for confirmation.

Neveah is taken back by his odd request, her eyes quickly scanning his outstretched hand and his smug smile before a playful smirk overtakes her once doubtful features. The Angel took his hand in a healthy handshake, their eyes locking as they sealed the deal.

"You're on, high roller."

"Don't hold your breath either, my lady."

CHAPTER 15

REALIZATIONS

ODESSA AND JAMES AZRAEL, the former King, and Queen of Heaven, sat idly in the council meeting as they awaited the presence of their new ruler along with the other members of high status. The circular room was organized in tiers, the sections broken up with slanted marble and gold which seated its prestigious members. In the center of the room, a single seat was raised above all the rest. The air in the room held a thickness to it, as a multitude of eyes scanned the bodies around them.

James and Odessa claimed each other's hand at the sound of the council room's door opening. It prompted every individual sitting to abruptly stand at their feet. From their seats, the duo watched as a serious and well-dressed Cassius Black made his entrance with his trusted advisor and military captain, Felix, at his side. Felix stops at the stairs leading up to the throne, as Cassius continues walking upwards until he is seated. He looks over everyone standing before him, a small smile clear on his features as he finally speaks to the collective.

"Please, my friends, be seated."

The elites obliged swiftly, sitting down as Cassius continued.

"I would like to thank you all for being here, first and foremost. As you are all aware, we suffered a tragic loss just a few weeks ago. A tragedy like this has not occurred in our realm for centuries and we are all shaken up by it. Our beloved Neveah Azrael took her own life on the day we were to be wed. It is a horrible and unfortunate occurrence, especially for her mother and father who sit with us today. I ask of you all to please pray for our former leaders in this trying time." Cassius gives a small nod in their direction, though his eyes never meet theirs. Instead, they hold no warmth, almost as if they were lifeless. He looks around the room, never making eye contact or resting his sight on anything. His cold cast eyes were always moving.

"We have not been able to resurrect her body from the water of the sea after days of trying, a truly tragic answer to her otherwise sinful actions." He says rather deeply, causing James to shift angrily in his seat. The duo was bewildered at Cassius' changed demeanor and seemingly unapologetic words on the throne.

"It saddens me that I will be leading this realm alone, though I hold with me the idea of our savior's divine plan. Everything happens for a reason, my friends—"

"—how dare you, Cassius!" James erupts from his seat, Odessa's eyes worriedly scanning from James to Cassius on the throne who looked amused by his outburst.

"You speak so coldly of our daughter, the rightful heir of the throne you so unmindfully sit upon. You should be ashamed of yourself! How can you be so smug when the woman that you loved is missing—"

"—dead." Cassius responds calmly, his face unwavering in emotion as he watches James and Odessa's light dim by the second.

James' voice cracks, his body shaking slightly as Odessa stands beside him finally.

"What...what did you just say?" He utters in disbelief as Cassius tilts his head at the couple.

"I said, she's dead."

Odessa wails at the confirmation, James is physically enraged by his nonchalant manner as he charges down the tier to reach Cassius upon his throne. Cassius looks down at the man in annoyance, fluttering his eyes as he clears his throat in attempts to continue the meeting. He sighed heavily as James began shouting up at him, his guards finally grabbing hold of the irate man and removing him from the room. A shattered Odessa chased after her husband as all eyes watched on in utter silence. Once the room was rid of Azrael's; Cassius shifted a bit in his seat before leveling his shoulders.

"Now, where were we?"

Cassius sat rather unamused at his new desk inside his very own office, the space very tidy and in pristine shape. He tapped a gold point pen on the white marble top of the desk, whistling slowly before his attention was forced towards the opening of the door to his office.

"Excuse me for disturbing you, my lord. I have the transcripts you sent for, along with the sacred text."

Cassius sat up straight, facing the scribe as he worriedly walked forward into the office and towards a waiting Cassius. He carefully handed the papers to Cassius, who took them without another word as he feverishly flipped open the first book within his reach.

"Anything else I can do or get for you before my departure, sir?"

Cassius, still enraptured in the words below him, simply waved the young man off in annoyance which only caused the scribe to scurry off just as quickly.

Cassius' sepia brown eyes scanned the various pages before him, books which were once banned and never to be touched, never alone opened—that is, until now. Cassius, almost in a frenzy, swiped the pages one after another as he indulged himself in the history of the realm below. Hell was indeed a ghoulish and evil place for mortals to be processed into, though how would it be for a mere Angel who knew nothing of the horrors of the world? This question kept gnawing at Cassius as he absorbed the information before him, the thought of Neveah still being alive left him in a torn mindset.

A part of him was very pleased and relieved of the idea that Neveah might still be alive—living and breathing. He did love her…or did he? The only reason he doubted the feeling was due to the dark and rather newfound emotion he experienced whilst sitting alone on the throne in the council meeting just hours before. The way everyone stood and bowed for him and him only. It was such a riveting and pleasurable experience—Cassius wasn't sure if he wanted to share it with anyone else.

The newfound King's thoughts came to a crashing halt as he stumbled across an unopened book. It was sealed on all four sides by crimson red wax, the ribbons nearly cracked and almost close to the end of its purpose. His hands carefully reached out, bringing the book in front of him. His wide hands held the book tightly, turning it over to admire its worn and rather dark looking cover. It stood out drastically against the rather innocent colors of white and gold of the room, even the shades of blue looked childish in comparison to the tough leather of the book he held in his palms.

Cassius curiously but carefully began to tear away the wax ribbons binding the book closed, his eyes hungry as they quickly danced along the frayed pages of the book—anxious to know what the leather cover held within its confides. It felt like forever for him, tearing away the frail wax bindings, but he was able to finally free the pages in a minute or so. He released a shaky breath, allowing his fear to show slightly as he opened the book with trembling digits. His eyes looked down warily before widening significantly. The pages were blank. He shuffled to the next one and the next one after that. He stopped for a second before ruffling the pages maniacally, dumbfounded at the sight of empty but worn pages.

He groaned in frustration, flitting the pages angrily before he stopped with a sharp outwards shout. He looked at his index finger, a cut blooming as blood rushed to the surface. The searing pain made him groan, making him shake his hand before placing his finger in his mouth in attempts to cease the bleeding. His face contorted in one of distaste upon realizing the apparent metal taste of blood. He removed his finger only to find the cut deepening, blood now steadily trickling from the wound. Cassius stood up quickly, both shocked and confused as he held his dripping finger over the book in astoundment.

Unnoticed to Cassius, in his frenzy and surprise from his worsening paper cut—his blood managed to drip onto the blank pages of the book below him. As he rushed to find anything to stop the bleeding, the book relished in the spatter as it suddenly came to life. The blood stains dissipated slowly as ink took its place on the once blank pages. Cassius did a double take upon seeing this, his sight just seeing his blood disappear before his eyes as the ink settled into the pages. He sat again, this time his face paled immensely as he watched the sight before him.

Holding onto his bleeding finger with a handkerchief, he acknowledged the fact that he couldn't understand the language. It was a hodgepodge of letters and symbols that looked so obscure, he couldn't possibly imagine what it all meant. He did his best to tie the handkerchief in place around his index finger before touching the page to turn it to the next. The symbols began to tremble, the ink shifting before his eyes as it suddenly became legible. Cassius let out a surprised gasp, his heart nearly beating out of his chest as he began to read the ancient-looking writing.

"What in heaven's name..." he uttered to himself, his brows scrunching as his chest felt so heavy suddenly.

The more Cassius seemed to read, the more irritable and chaotic his mind would feel. The King hadn't even finished reading the first two pages of the book before he was interrupted by his squire. The knocking at his door fell on deaf ears as he greedily read through the writing, unbeknownst to his squire who entered quietly.

"My lord?"

Cassius looked crazed sitting behind his very unorganized desk, his handkerchief finger almost soaked all the way through with his blood as his face was nearly buried in the pages of the book. The squire ventured forth carefully, calling for him again to no answer. Cassius' heart nearly stopped at the last sentence of the page, his frame shaking from disbelief before he looked up in a whirl. The squire had nearly shouted for his attention, meeting the older man's crazed eyes as he stepped back in fear.

"M-my deepest apologies, sir. You've been called to the council room. The Azrael's would like a word with you in private."

Cassius' heavy breathing and rather unhinged state frightened the young squire, his eyes wide as he tried to read the King. Cassius swallowed the lump in his throat, doing his best to steady his breathing as he wiped at his sweaty forehead with his sleeve.

"I'll be out in a moment. Uh," he began, before he finally registered the worsening state of his finger.

"—call the doctor as well." Cassius said, looking at the saturated cloth around his skin.

The squire went to speak again but quieted quickly, his body jumping at the King's abrupt movements as he rose from his seated position and stalked out of the room.

"Keep standing there looking lost. I'll do it myself." He uttered rudely with his departure, leaving the young man in shock as he stood frozen in his spot.

Once Cassius was out of sight, the squire looked back towards the exit cautiously and then towards the open book on his desk. With one final look at the door, he quickly but quietly made his way closer to the desk. Looking back for any sign of someone entering, he then carefully looked over the desk and at the pages of the open book.

The squire's brows immediately furrowed, shaking his head as he became obviously confused. He turned then, walking out of the room slowly as he registered what he just saw—a worn book with only blank pages.

CHAPTER 16

LOVE CAN KILL

CASSIUS HAD MADE A feverish entrance into the rather empty council room. He looked quite ill, his face a sickly pale and a clear sheen of sweat beading his forehead. His hands still trembled from before, the notion rather obvious as he tried to damp away the sweat upon his forehead. His wounded finger was now bandaged professionally by the medic, the skin wrapped skillfully with white gauze and tape. It appeared rather gaudy in comparison to his very royal and grandeur appearance.

Cassius walked toward The Azrael's in a mix of frustration and annoyance, his two royal guards flanking either side of him as he stopped a mere few feet from the distressed couple. It was clear that the two had been crying, their eyes puffed, and red rimmed as James stood to his feet with ferocity. He had begun to take a few steps forward towards Cassius but was quickly redirected as the royal guards took his arms in restraint.

"You two are becoming quite troublesome, it's rather distasteful for your status. I expected more from the two of you...especially you, James. You led our realm with great faith and strength once upon a time, though now it seems that you've regressed into a state of cowardice. How is that?"

"You are a disgrace to all that is good, Cassius. How dare you treat us with such indifference? How could you say what you said about our beloved Nevaeh? She cared about you!"

"Did she?! Oh, heavens, please forgive me for missing that sentiment. I'm afraid she never said that to me, because if she did, I do believe she would be beside me at this moment."

"Cassius, please...have mercy..." Odessa sobbed, reaching outwards towards Cassius as he continued to stand idle.

"Mercy? It seems my mercy ran out when your daughter decided to kill herself to leave my side."

James screamed in anger, continuing to thrash to get to Cassius but to no avail.

"What was it that you beckoned me for? I'm a very busy man."

"The lord sees your intentions—he sees the malice and dishonor in your heart. That's why you look so ill. You will reap what you sow, Cassius Black. How could you be this way...it isn't morally right."

"Morally, right? You shouldn't discuss what is and isn't morally right, with a daughter who committed the worst atrocity of the realm. She broke the number one rule—yet I still have the mercy you claim I do not have by not punishing you both

for her crime. You will look upon me with gratitude, Azrael's—
"

"—you are no king. How dare you even walk around here and preach about love, sanctity, and faith when you cannot even mourn the loss of your loved one. You are shameful!" Odessa cries loudly, collapsing a few feet before Cassius who merely looked down at her scornfully.

"As your king, I demand you tell me what this is all about. I have duties to fulfill and won't stand by to enable this ghastly behavior. What is it that the two of you want?"

"We want you to find our daughter, Cassius! Our little girl is somewhere in the water, and we need her back home!" Odessa sobs, James finally shaking the guards away as he stumbled backwards to meet Odessa's crumpled body on the ground.

"Well, it seems that I cannot fulfill your request. We searched for three days and found no remnants of your daughter. Therefore, it is a waste of my resources to keep my men looking for something that isn't there. Will that be all?"

"Damn you, damn you to hell, Cassius. Satan would be grateful to have you."

"Is that so?" Cassius responds in a deadpan manner, looking at both his guards before they violently grab James and begin to pull him away from Odessa's slumped and screaming body on the floor.

She desperately tries to grip James' legs as they pull him away, her outstretched hands meeting the polished shoes of Cassius.

She looks up in fear, his eyes holding no emotion whatsoever as he gives a carefree smile.

"Now, what'll I do with you?"

Later, that evening, Cassius could be seen unhinged. His room was nearly in shambles, with books and papers thrown astray. His bedding and curtains nearly torn from their respected places in a fit of rage and disbelief. His clothing was untidy and clearly worn, his hair a disheveled mess as it easily frayed over his eyes. His sweat began to show through his white linen dress shirt, which was now almost completely undone. He shakily held a single piece of paper in his right hand and another in his left, as he held them side by side.

His eyes vivaciously danced over the writing of the pages before he tossed them in the air. He nearly tripped over the mess to get back to his desk opposite of the room, his unsteady hands gripping the ancient text from Hell. He had stopped his reading before as he recalled the feeling of imminent danger along with evil overwhelming emotions he couldn't place. Though Cassius was desperate to find answers to where Nevaeh could have gone.

Though the man seemed so blasé about the situation, a part of him needed to find the reasoning behind her disappearance. Disappearance, as in he knew she wasn't dead. He had such a strong feeling in his gut which reinforced the fact she was alive—if not here, then most certainly down there. As Cassius continued to read the sinister text, he began to see distorted visions. He shouted in a mix of panic and pain, closing his eyes as he tried to calm himself down. He screamed in agony again, his knees colliding with the crumpled mess of books and paper below as he held his head in anguish.

These visions—they were violent. He saw executions of screaming individuals. So much fire, so much blood. It was like he was suffocating from the smell of smoke and death, his eyes nearly red from his strain to breathe normally. Then he had saw something rather peculiar. It seemed to be a rather desolate area, with ravaged trees and no sign of life. Though in the distance, he saw a barrier of bloodied stakes with decaying skulls. He seemed to transport through the black rusted gate and into a dodgy and menacing looking village until he looked up and towards a rusted red door. He had heard a melodious voice from the other side, it was rather surprised and even concerning— "who are you?"

Cassius then gasped for air, falling over as he began coughing deeply. He tried his hardest to catch his breath, his lungs wheezing from the immense struggle as he carefully brings the book up so he can read the remaining passage of the last page. At the top, the boldface letters caught his attention entirely as he said the words out loud.

"The Prophecy."

CHAPTER 17

WELCOME TO PARADISE

NEVAEH HAD BEEN BUSY enjoying the company of Lennox for the past week with the Blood Ball drawing nearby. Their days were filled with countless fittings and the creation of Nevaeh's new closet filled to the brim with clothes fit for the queen she would become. The angel saw Damien once or twice in the past few days, which was unfortunate for the pair. The two would look at one another in that short moment with a mix of longing and sorrow, their apologetic eyes unbeknownst to everyone else around them.

It was a rather calm day for the artist and his muse, the duo taking a break in the grandiose fashion studio. Lennox had stepped out of the room for a few minutes, leaving Nevaeh alone with her own thoughts. She kept thinking about Damien and what he might be up to. She couldn't get him out of her head. She was nervous about seeing him again after all these days. What would she say to him? She felt so childish. Her fingers picked at the fraying fabric of the lace in her corset, the deep plum color striking against her olive toned skin. She looked off at nothing, allowing her thoughts to roam freely. A round of knocks nearly kicked her back into real time as she whipped her head fiercely to the sound, only to become relieved at the sound of Lennox's friendly voice. "Lady Nevaeh, are you decent?"

"Yes, you can come in." Lennox entered smoothly then, in his grasp a velveteen box which was rectangular in shape. It immediately caught her eye, as the velvet was an emerald green. It reminded her of Damien's eyes. She had wished to see them up close again so desperately. Lennox wore a sly smirk, watching Nevaeh nearly become entranced by the box he held in his hand.

"What's that?" She inquired casually, though her voice held a certain curiosity for it.

"It's a gift," he began, holding in flat in both his palms as he kneeled to her seated position on the steps leading up to the small fitting stage.

Nevaeh's eyes widened a bit as her heartbeat increased, her eyes leveling with Lennox's hazel eyes. "…King Damien asked me to give this to you on his behalf. He apologizes for being so fleeting in your meetings and overall, in his absence. He's been quite busy with the elites and planning for the Blood Ball. He is hoping to see you this evening for dinner if you'd accept his offer."

Nevaeh carefully reached forward, allowing her fingers to softly graze the velvet of the box before opening it carefully. She had gasped lowly, her mouth agape as she carefully reached for the beautiful necklace placed neatly on the black silk place holder. It was the most elegant piece of jewelry she'd ever seen, a thin gold chain with a single emerald gemstone at the end. It gleamed even in the low light of the studio, which amazed Nevaeh. "Wow." She breathed, holding the gemstone in her palm before looking up to an almost beaming Lennox.

"D'you like it?" He asks softly, causing Nevaeh to nod quickly as she finally allowed a bashful smile to cross her face.

"He didn't have to do this; it is so beautiful." She motions for Lennox to place it around her neck. "Do you mind?"

Lennox smiled in response, carefully taking the necklace, and standing to place the jewelry around her neck. She helps him as she grasps her curly hair upward so he can see better. She closed her eyes upon having the clasp touch her skin, signaling it was now safe around her neck. Lennox stepped forward into her line of sight again, clasping his hands together. "You look radiant, Nevaeh."

"Did he say anything else?" She quipped, eager to know any extra details Lennox had left out regarding his brief encounter with the King. "No, only to report back to him if you accepted his invitation for dinner. Also, for you to be ready by six o'clock this evening." Nevaeh smiled, playing with the emerald pendant at the end of her necklace. "What should I wear?" she asked, almost in a daze as Lennox rolled his eyes playfully. "You leave that to me."

Damien tried his hardest to keep his composure as he sat at the head of the large conference table in the meeting room of the main hall of the castle. A room full of bickering and opinionated elites sat before him as they gathered to discuss everything they couldn't at the past Black Ball. Damien did his best to seem concerned, but his façade was slowly dropping. "Your highness, it seems as though you've allowed the renegade division to fester and become a true subsidiary in the realm. How can we successfully run our cities and keep our damned in line when these hellions are snatching them left and right?!"

Damien went to speak but was quickly replaced with another elite who added to their concerns. "I absolutely agree. We are losing sight of the realm's rules and regulations. This newfound division is dangerous, even to us. If they continue to grow, they'll become too powerful to stop. Morana is as unpredictable as she is vicious. She won't stop until she gets what she wants."

"And that is?" Damien inquired pointedly as he sat in straight in his seat.

The elites look at one another warily, before one of them cleared their throat before continuing.

"Isn't it obvious, sir? I mean, why would the daughter of a high-status leader rebel against the crown who shaped her? She's angry and she wants one of two things—maybe even both,"

"—and you think so poorly of the crown? Of myself? I should try you for treason for you to even think of that as a possibility." Damien said strongly, causing the elites to quiet down significantly.

"Sir—" the man began before Damien quieted him down once more.

"—enough, Rick. I don't want to hear anything more from a spy renegade like yourself. How about you give Morana my regards and let her know I'll be looking forward to seeing her soon." Damien said rather nonchalantly, though his eyes gave away his true feelings of anger. The King snapped his fingers, making the table of elites jump in their seats for a millisecond before they regained their composure. It was then that Damien's guards moved in, grabbing Rick from his seat forcefully by the collar of his blood red button-down shirt.

The middle-aged man tried his best to fight back, as every other member of the table averted their gaze from his struggle. He called out to them, pleading for them to do something, before he spoke to Damien. His mouth full of blood and his attire completely disheveled as he continued to fight with his guards. Damien's face never changed, his features still—cold—as he watched Rick become a spectacle of the room.

"You'll wish you never did this, Damien. You'll be begging for mercy once Morana rules the realm and rids it of all your soft-minded cretin. We'll start with that angel bitch that made you forget what we're really here for—" Rick then spits at Damien, his blood creating a morbid maroon spatter design across the marble table.

Damien smirked, his eyes leveling as he carefully stood from his seated position. He adjusted his black suit jacket with sangfroid, looking at all the other elites at the table before walking over to Rick. The guards held him in place, his heaving chest exciting to Damien as he reveled in his bubbling fear as he drew closer. Rick tried to hide it, his bloodied smile and shaky laughter enough to give him away. Damien smiled at him, a glimmer of amusement in his eyes as he lifted his hand only to have Rick flinch.

Damien saw this, marinating in the electricity of the moment before he pinched at his bottom lip. He then at once reached forward and grabbed his jaw, gripping forcefully as he looked down at him.

"Since you want to act like the boss, I'll treat you as such. Then, during your last breath, you'll tell Morana why I mutilated you beyond belief. Me? I don't care much about slander or disrespect; I handle it as I should. Though, you messed up when you mentioned someone you know nothing about. So, you'll be my first and hopefully only example of what happens when you disrespect the crown and its leading lady."

The guards then forcefully drag Rick out of the room, his shouts echoing in the otherwise quiet room. Damien slicks his hair back coolly, his rings still glistening in the dim lit room. He gives a slight knowing grin at the frozen elites.

"I'm sure you all learned a valuable lesson at this evening's meeting. I would spread the word to the others to keep me from losing my temper, you know? We wouldn't want that, hm?"

They immediately agreed, clearing their throats, and nodding simultaneously as they did their best to smile to hide their bubbling fear. Damien closed his eyes for a moment and sighed, before smiling wide. It caused crinkles at this corner of his eyes, his emerald, green orbs nearly glistening as he tapped one of the elites on their shoulder reassuringly.

"I want reports of the renegade divisions infiltration in each sector before the blood ball. I need to know what we're dealing with when the party arrives. Other than that, I appreciate you all for coming out."

He whistled an old tune as he exited the meeting room, the small group of elites still frozen in place but able to breathe once Damien was out of sight. They hadn't said a word to one another, their crazed eyes enough to convey what they were all feeling and thinking in that exact moment—The King of Hell was not to ever be messed with.

Nevaeh's heart raced as she sat in her seat at the circular dinner table where she waited for Damien's arrival. The dinner was set outside on the west wing's patio due to its view. It was spectacular yet daunting to say the least, Nevaeh was taken away by the bright orange and reds that dipped through the sky. It was almost sundown, the sky providing a gorgeous orange glowing cast to everything its light touched. It made Nevaeh's skin radiant against the dark emerald green of her flowing gown. She was nervous to have worn this specific piece, fearing it would be too revealing for a dinner with the king. Lennox talked her out of her head, reassuring her that he would love it and that it paired beautifully with her new necklace. She shuddered suddenly at the brisk wind that passed over her, her exposed back littering in small goosebumps at the shift in temperature. She sighed, looking around the otherwise empty space beside the few guards before standing at her feet. Her silk gown billowed for just a moment as she moved towards the stone railing to peer over its edge.

Her brown curls blew astray in the warm breeze, her eyes closing briefly as she breathed in. The familiar scent of warmth enveloped her senses immediately as she smirked to herself— burning wood, a hint of smoke, and leather? Nevaeh's eyes shot open as she turned quickly, bracing herself along the railing as she met Damien's wandering eyes. How? She had thought immediately only to be answered with a smug smirk from the tall man before her.

"I thought you might like the view."

She didn't answer him, still staring at him like a deer in headlights. She was very confused. She could usually feel him when he was close, but now she felt nothing. She tugged her brows together, giving him a puzzled look before his smile dropped.

"Everything alright?" he asked seriously, slowly walking closer, so he stood about a foot in front of her.

"I…I'm not sure." she answered honestly, tucking hair behind her ear as she pushed herself off the railing and walked up to meet him. He looked down at her with a mix of emotion. Longing, admiration, curiosity, fear…

"I couldn't feel you…I didn't even know you were here."

Damien felt a pang in his chest hearing her voice waver. Was she upset? His plan had backfired it seemed.

"That would be my doing, actually."

She looked up at him, her eyes wide in surprise as her mouth fell agape.

"How? Why?" she asked lowly as she searched his eyes for an answer before he spoke.

Damien carefully reached up, pressing gently against the emerald gemstone between her clavicle with pristine focus. Her brown eyes never left his.

"I thought you'd be happier without the extra sensory issues. Medici conjured up a spell that halts the connection when you wear this."

"Wow…" she breathed, touching the stone softly as she looked down at it again in wonder. "That's very thoughtful of you. I thought something happened to me."

He snickered, shaking his head in amusement before softly grazing the silk that covered her arm. He trailed down to her wrist, grabbing her hand softly which nearly caused Nevaeh to go weak in the knees. He had never touched her hand before. The act was so intimate yet childish, she felt embarrassed for feeling so enthused by his action. He began to lead her back to her seat, their hands separating as Damien pulled her seat out for her to sit. She obliged shyly, thanking him quietly before he sat opposite her at the table. She was silent as she watched him get comfortable, rolling his shoulders and letting out a breath he seemed to be holding onto forever. He undid his cufflinks, rolling his sleeves up casually as Nevaeh nearly spaced out at the sight of him doing something so normal.

He noticed her rather blank stare immediately but let her revel in the moment rather than make fun of her. He had all night to do that.

"My Lord, My Lady," A new voice spoke rather enthusiastically, causing Damien to tug his brows together in distaste.

Upon seeing the king's reaction, the nearing chef cleared his throat and reevaluated his approach.

"What might I get started for you both? Any drinks?"

Nevaeh looked over to Damien quickly, becoming nervous at the simple question. Damien, in contrast, leaned back a bit and pondered the question for a second before answering.

"I'll just have bourbon neat. Some water too. Nevaeh?"

She opened her mouth, but nothing came out, Damien laughed lightly, trying to make her comfortable as he sensed her growing anxiety.

"I think she's good with water for now. Thanks, T."

He gave her a reassuring smile before tilting his head slightly in curiosity. Nevaeh averted her gaze, turning her focus to the view over the railing before he spoke up.

"You're nervous. Why?"

Nevaeh shook her head, trying her best to look genuine.

"No, I'm fine."

"Your heart is racing."

Her face fell at his words, her eyes then narrowing as she looked at him.

"How do you know that?"

"I'm not wearing a necklace." He whispered comically, his smile nearly dazzling as her cheeks visibly turned pink.

She groaned and placed her face in her hands in embarrassment as Damien pursed his lips at her reaction. The chef appeared again, placing the drinks on the table silently as Nevaeh removed her hands and thanked the man as he poured her water. He looked surprised at her politeness, making her second-guess the gesture. She apologized immediately but Damien shook his head, trying to reassure her. In attempts to ease her nerves, he also thanked the chef, which caused the man to nearly spill the water he was pouring. She laughed almost instantly, covering her mouth as Damien gave her a knowing look. He nodded at Chef T before he nearly scurried off.

"You actually said 'thank you' to someone. I feel like you've reached a major milestone in your life."

"I've said it before."

"Oh yeah? When was the last time?"

The duo let the silence envelope them, but it wasn't at all awkward. It was amusing, as the two tried their hardest not to let a smile spread across their faces.

"Fine, it's been a while."

"Well maybe you should say it more. It makes people feel good when you thank them. They feel seen when you do."

"Noted."

The two fell into a comfortable silence before Nevaeh continued the conversation without missing a beat.

"How have you been these past two weeks? Everything okay with work?'

Damien sat up in his seat a bit more, leaning a bit onto the table as he answered her.

"I've been alright, considering the insane amount of nagging from Davina about The Blood Ball and all the problems with this newfound renegade division in the south. Everything has just been a clusterfuck of madness. I'm sorry we couldn't talk or meet during this whole thing. I've just been pulled in every direction."

"No need to apologize. I know you have a lot of responsibilities to take care of. Important matters are always first." Nevaeh smiled as she reached for her glass.

"You're important as well, Nevaeh. Don't misconstrue my words."

She stopped for a second before nodding once.

"Thank you." She said pointedly, referencing her earlier statement as he made a sound in realization.

"Now I see what you mean." He replied, taking a sip of the dark liquor in his stout glass before continuing. "How about you? Has everyone been accommodating?"

Nevaeh nodded quickly, swallowing her cold water before answering. "Yes, most definitely. I've spent a lot of my time in the library. I think it's my second favorite place in the castle, aside from the secret garden," she smiles at him, making him return the favor as she continues. "—I've been able to learn a bit more about the realm and its history with whatever books I could find. Lennox and Medici have also been great with helping me understand anything I had questions of, well when they had time, of course."

"So, what have you learned? Let's test your knowledge."

Nevaeh chuckles, shaking her hands in protest.

"No way, I can't remember everything off the top of my head."

"What's one thing you found most interesting then?"

Nevaeh hummed in thought, tapping the black silk cloth of the table as she crossed her legs under the table.

"Probably the way the realm is split into different sectors or divisions based on their crime. I always thought it was somewhat of a chaotic free-for-all down here, well, that's what we're taught to believe."

"Yeah, well, even us sinners need a little bit of structure. We aren't complete animals."

"Also learned a bit about you."

"Is that so? Learned everything you need to know in a dusty textbook in a cursed library?"

Nevaeh stilled, her voice lowering as she looked concerned. "The library is haunted?" She inquires nervously as Damien allows a genuine laugh to bounce between them.

"No, I don't know, I was just joking," He continued through a light string of laughter as she rolled her eyes playfully.

"Well, I learned a bit about how you process souls. It's actually very different from how Heaven does it. We just welcome everyone who appears at the gates, well, my mom and dad did. No questions asked, just…acceptance. Here, you question them—make them relive their crimes. If you feel they can be useful to you, you change them into hill demons or a stygian. If they're far beyond your judgement, you'll place them into a specific division based on their crimes where they're said to suffer and work relentlessly under the rule of the division's elite leader."

"Something like that, sure."

"Is that not really it? Maybe the text was outdated."

"No, you've got it down basically. Just…sometimes things don't go exactly as planned. I don't have a handbook when I process the bastards. Things can get a little messy."

Nevaeh furrows her brow at his words, not necessarily liking how he phrased his answer but couldn't respond as Chef T reappeared with an entourage and dinner. His assistants placed an array of plates around the table, prompting Damien to grab a cloth and shake it out to place on his lap. Nevaeh surveyed the many options of food before her, smiling as she realized that some of these items looked familiar. She couldn't help the tears that sprung to her eyes at the realization that these were some of her favorite foods and snacks. She looked up at Chef T, her eyes glistening as he smiled back at her. He clasped his hands together once his assistants placed down all the items.

"My Lord, My Lady. A dinner for two, celebrating two realms coming together. For Hell's delicacies, we have a mix of wildfire vegetables pan seared and roasted, filet mignon medium rare basted with onyx pepper butter, and a grand spread of mashed potatoes made from umber speckled spuds. Representing Heaven, we have delicate cloud cakes prepared with an assortment of whipped butters and cream, a special rendition of pates delicates with a garnish of toasted clovers, as well as a simple yet delectable honey-grain baguette with a generous meadow-herb spread."

Nevaeh couldn't hold back the choked sob that wracked her body before she covered her face. Everyone stilled, Nevaeh's body shaking slightly as she cried silently. Chef T stood awkwardly frozen in place as Damien stood, his chair scraping against the marble floor as he came to her side. He kneeled, carefully touching her shoulder before reaching for her wrists.

"Nevaeh,"

She shook her head, her hands still covering her face as he nodded at Chef T for him to leave them alone.

"Hey…don't cry, Vae." Damien said softly, causing her to drop her hands from her face to look at him. The sight made his heart tinge, seeing her so upset caused his face to fall almost immediately.

"I'm sorry—" she gasped, going to cover her face again but was stopped by Damien's grasp. She looked away from him, her embarrassment bubbling over as she closed her eyes.

"Don't be sorry. It's me that should be apologizing. I didn't think this would make you upset, I thought the opposite." He tried to lighten the mood with a breathless chuckle. He softly wipes away at her freckled cheeks, her tears wet against his hot touch as she seemed to calm at his actions.

"I had asked Lennox what foods you were missing from home, and he was able to somehow get you to talk about it. I figured you'd feel more comfortable if you had something that reminded you of home."

Nevaeh turned to look at him now, her hands going to his shoulders as he gave a trying smile.

"I can make them take it away, you know that."

She shook her head, smirking at him before sniffling.

"No, that would be very rude, Damien."

"It upset you."

"No, it made me so happy. I couldn't believe it; I was just surprised. I'm humiliated now because I cried in front of you and T over food." She chuckled then, groaning before wiping her eyes. Damien reached over and handed her a napkin, allowing her to dab at her eyes more easily. He then stood, reaching again to claim her skinny glass of water before holding it in front of her to grasp.

"Thanks."

He hummed in response, turning to walk back to his seat before watching her warily.

"I'm fine. I promise. I'm excited to try everything."

A few hours passed, with dinner being completed and countless words and laughter shared between the king and angel. The sun had set long ago, the duo now basked in a mix of candlelight and fire. The deep navy-black sky was littered with a multitude of tiny specs of light. Nevaeh had barely touched her dessert, which was rare for her. Damien had undone the top few buttons of his shirt, his hair tousled, and cheeks tinted a slight shade of pink from his bourbon. Nevaeh, too, was becoming a little restless but wouldn't show it. She was enjoying the time she had with Damien, as he was with her.

"You just told me you've never been to a concert. That's literally disgraceful. How can you have never heard music played live?"

"I have, Damien. Once, but that was from outside of the town hall." Nevaeh laughed at herself, her laughter falling in synch with Damien's as he hit the table a few times.

"Now I have to make some calls and get a concert going, just for you, My Lady."

"Oh no, don't call me that! It makes me sound like a thousand years old."

"Are you not a-thousand-and-one? Could've fooled me."

"Very funny, Mr. Devil-Man."

"Man...what time is it even? I think we may have over did it." He says deeply and Nevaeh nods.

"Yeah, seems like it. The sky says so at least."

Damien admires Nevaeh from his seat, his eyes raking over the semi-flushed skin of her face down to her blushed lips. He bit down on his lower lip on instinct, immediately thinking of how her kisses tasted like. He was sure it was the bourbon allowing him to think this freely, but it wasn't like he never thought of this before. He almost kissed her near the stairs of the garden those few weeks ago. It was almost electrifying to think about it, he raised a brow to himself as he sighed and stood. He pushed the thought aside and focused on the moment.

"Alright party animal. I'll walk you to your room."

Nevaeh pouted then, making Damien nearly double over in pain. God, how he wanted to kiss her. Again, he pushed the invasive thought aside. He knew what could happen if he went for it, and was afraid that once he started, he wouldn't know how to stop.

"I'm not even tired." She playfully whispered only to have him slowly walk over to her with a lopsided smirk.

"You need to rest. You have lessons starting tomorrow."

"Lessons? What for?"

"Oh man...they didn't tell you?"

Nevaeh seemed to sober up immediately, though Damien kept his lighthearted demeanor and sloppy grin.

"What are you talking about?" She sputtered and he reached forward for her, pulling her up from her seat.

The pair stood close, their bodies touching as Damien's hands reached down to grab her hands to position them in place. Nevaeh gasped as it dawned on her, the pair standing in a perfect tango position.

"No— "she groaned in agony as Damien did his best to not laugh.

"Oh yes. It's a tradition to do a waltz at the Blood Ball. It's what gets the party started."

"Just kill me now, please— "she nearly cried as Damien spun her out in surprise. She shrieked, holding his hand out as he smiled.

"See? You're a natural."

"I can't dance, Damien."

"Neither do I. I just have all the moves memorized." He winks, pulling her in so her back is pressed against his front. Damien's arms stayed wrapped around her chest, swaying the two of them carefully before he slowly stepped backwards. It was then that he was able to fully see her dress for what it was—or what it wasn't. Her bare back was on display, her gorgeous skin kissed with a sprinkling of beauty marks and freckles which matched the ones on her face. He blinked slowly, carefully reaching out to graze his fingertips against her bare skin. The action made her jump, his touch retreating before reaching forward again.

"Lennox said the dress was symbolic to emotion. You cover up what you want people to see, putting on a put together façade; but when you turn your back, you unravel, allowing your true nature to show."

"Thank you, Lennox." He says lowly, clearly amused by her attempts to keep calm.

"He said you'd love it."

He whistles lowly in response, featherlight tracing the outline of her spine down to her lower back where he tapped an unknown rhythm.

"Lennox has always been an honest man."

His touch left her burning skin, his warmth fading as she turned to see why. Damien was grabbing his jacket, putting it back on with one swift movement before prompting her to follow him out. They walked rather close to one another, going over dinner and seeing how much they both enjoyed each other's company. It was obvious that neither of them wanted the night to end, the pair using any excuse not to say goodnight.

"We should thank T for dinner. You think he's still up?"

"Maybe. Though he's probably tired from all the prepping and catering from today so maybe not."

Nevaeh nodded in understanding, placing her hands behind her back as she stood tall. Damien leaned against the wall beside her door, watching her become anxious with each passing second.

"Will I be seeing you tomorrow?"

"That all depends. Would you like to see me tomorrow?"

"Sure. That would be nice. That is, if you have time for me."

Damien chuckles lowly, pushing himself off the wall so he stands in front of her.

"I'll always have time for you, Vae."

Her heart nearly stopped; his smirk devilish as he picked up on that immediately.

"That's not fair." She whispered when she realized his tactic.

"I like making you blush. Your heart racing is just the icing on the cake."

"Oh, whatever." She grumbled, their faces mere inches from one another before Damien smirked deviously.

"Goodnight, angel." He pulled away, taking a couple steps back as he indirectly prompted her to go into her room.

He could see the disappointment on her face; she wanted him to kiss her. He would've if it were anyone else, though Nevaeh wasn't just anyone else. He wanted her, he absolutely wanted to. He just wanted it to be perfect, he wanted the moment to be special. She deserved that much.

"Goodnight, Devil-Man." She joked, trying to smile to hide her sadness.

He smiled one last time at her silly name for him, taking a few steps backward.

"Sleep well." He stated finally, turning as she opened the door to her room.

"You too." She said but realized she had answered too late. The hallway was now empty. She looked longingly down to hall, for a moment she felt like being rash and brazen even. She felt like running after him and kissing the life out of him.

She desperately wanted his hands on her skin again. She looked down, shaking her head as if to rid her brain of the idea. She took a deep breath and entered her room in defeat.

CHAPTER 18

NOCTURNAL WALTZ

SPINE-CHILLING SCREAMS AND CRIES were the only sounds filling the dimly lit dungeon as Damien watched the stygian torture firsthand. The creatures were ruthless, leaving Rick a bloodied mess but just coherent enough for him to recognize Damien's arrival. He gasped for air, his head lulling to the side as his arms were bound on either side of his head. He hung just a few inches from the ground, his beaten body on display through his heavily soiled open red shirt. Damien entered casually, Dante behind him as he stood tall by the entrance. Damien carefully took off his suit jacket, handing it to Dante who gave him a knowing look. It wasn't so much of a warning, but more of a reminder—*remember who you are*. Damien then continued to roll his black sleeves up, sniffling as he tried to mute Rick begging for forgiveness.

"Damien, my king, please forgive me. I was enchanted, I had no idea what I was doing. Morana is dangerous, she's pure evil. Please, my lord, have mercy." He cried, his sobs echoing off the wall as Damien walked closer to his hanging body.

Damien pushed him slightly, causing him to wince in pain, his relentless begging jumbling together and sounding like gibberish. Damien then stared at his face for a minute. He began to remember his threat at the meeting earlier which only seemed to send him into a blazing rage; especially after the night he had just spent with Neveah. Damien had wound his fist back with immense fury, contacting Rick's nose with a demeaning crack that sent him screaming. Damien moved back and around his swaying body, his eyes dark as he watched him struggle to breathe.

"I told you I'd send you back unrecognizable. Did you think I was bluffing?"

Dante had looked down, the scene before him a little too surreal and frightening to witness in real time. The stygian guards watched eagerly in the shadows, waiting for an order to continue their vicious assault on their prisoner.

It seemed like hours passed in that small dungeon cell as Damien wreaked havoc upon Rick's body. It had left him shirtless and sweaty, an absolutely frightening bloodied mess as he continued his assault on his humanoid punching bag. Rick had passed out just a moment ago, Damien's torso and forearms almost completely saturated with this man's blood. His chest heaved, his hands pushing his hair back feverishly as he wiped his face of sweat and blood spatter only to make his features more morbid in appearance. He shook his hands out, blood nearly dripping from his fingertips before placing them on his hips as he watched Rick's nearly lifeless body sway slightly. He shook his pockets briefly, reaching into his right pocket to grab a slim box of his onyx cigarettes. He placed one between his lips with a huff, reaching in the direction of Dante who rested his armored body against the entry way facing out instead of in at the horror.

"You got a light, D?" He rasped, breathless from his previous onslaught as Dante slowly turned and did his best not to look at the mess he made. It was highly difficult, being that Damien was nearly covered head to toe in it. Dante took his lighter from his chest pocket, holding it out as he lit Damien's bloodied cigarette. He snapped the silver top closed with a clink, prompting Damien to take a long inhale of the stick's smoke before blowing a hard line of smoke into the dark room. Dante cleared his throat, leveling his eyes with Damien's closed ones before he opened them slowly to meet his stern gaze.

"What now?"

Damien smirked manically, tapping his shoulder strongly with one hand as he took a drag out of his cigarette with his other.

"We send this fucker back to his leader."

Nevaeh was becoming increasingly frustrated as she twirled around the grand and very spacious ballroom alone with Davina's shouting instruction. She had managed to stumble and trip over herself a few times, a mixture of missteps and courtesy of her lace gown. She groaned when Davina prompted her to stop for what seemed like the hundredth time to start from the top of the routine.

"You're stiff like a board. Loosen up, Nevaeh!" She nearly croaked, causing the angel to hang her head in defeat.

"I need a partner to practice with. It's the only way I'm really going to get a feel for this."

Davina shook her head, pointing to Quinn who sat aside while Medici tended to his burned hands. "We tried that princess, look where it got us."

"Can't he wear gloves or something? I just need someone to help guide me—"

"—I am guiding you! Is my voice not carrying through to you? AGAIN!" Davina exclaimed as she promoted the tired pianist to start the score from the beginning with a round of feverish snaps.

Nevaeh took a deep breath and did her best to focus on what she's learned. She had stepped rather gracefully along to the melody, her arms taking place behind her as she twirled and dipped to the rhythm. Davina's voice continued to coach her through the piano's strong sound, slicing through to help her reach the next move with precision. Nevaeh, too focused on the routine and Davina's tough instruction, continued to dance with her eyes closed so she hadn't noticed a new person join their strict rehearsal.

"Fantastic job, flow into the next portion—don't think about the steps as much. You know them well enough."

This was always the part that Nevaeh messed up, a part that required a partner and she always missed her cue. Davina felt the error coming, about to stop the music and Nevaeh from becoming upset again before the angel turned swiftly into his body. Her eyes shot open upon impact, reaching out to balance herself as he too grabbed hold of her arms to keep her upright. She breathed quicker now, her face turning pink with embarrassment before she visibly calmed under Damien's strong touch and intense green eyes.

"Can't you see we're busy, Damien? I mean, seriously, are you that dense? The Ball is in a week, and she can't even get the simple steps down. We can't have any distractions; this is madness!"

Nevaeh fisted his suit jacket in frustration at Davina's tough words before Damien smoothed the skin of her arms softly in reassurance.

"She's going to learn it, Dav. I'm here to help."

"Fine, have it your way. I'll just sit aside with the wounded, no big deal."

Damien rolls his eyes, then furrows his brows once he realizes she wasn't exaggerating. Quinn gives a trying smile before Damien turns his attention toward a timid Nevaeh.

"You really must've been struggling to ask Quinn for assistance." He joked lightly, only for her to continue to look down.

"Hey," he carefully reached down and tilts her face up to meet his.

"We've got this. It's just a few steps here and there. Let's do it together."

Damien looks over to the tired looking pianist with expectation, causing the older man to perk up immediately as he began to play the song again. Nevaeh thought she had passed out, as the thought of her being this close to Damien was only her deepest secret, one she longed to come true. She kept her eyes level with his chest, focusing on the shiny black buttons of his button-down shirt as she did her best to calm her racing thoughts and heartbeat. She had gasped once she mis-stepped, but Damien quickly played it off as nothing as Davina clapped her hands.

"Was that a mistake? We will start over!" She warned loudly as Damien chuckled lowly, rolling his eyes over at Davina while the pair continued to dance around smoothly.

"You want us both skinned alive, huh? She's out for blood, Vae. Just follow my lead."

Nevaeh nods meekly, finally looking up into his eyes as he gave a faint smirk in reply.

"One and two and two and three and—Damien! We are not free styling!" Davina nearly screamed, going to walk over to the pair before Medici stopped her with a firm grab of her upper arm. She tugs angrily before he gives her a knowing look, then slowly moves to look over to Damien and Nevaeh. She follows his gaze, slowly releasing the tension in her body as he releases his firm grip. The two seemed to glide effortlessly around the room, almost like they were floating.

"The angel was right." She sighed, crossing her arms as she continued to watch on silently.

Nevaeh braced herself for the upcoming part of the routine, the part she had continuously messed up due to her lack of a partner. She nearly thought her heart stopped as Damien lifted her effortlessly off her feet, swaying her around for a moment before placing her down for a dip. Nevaeh did her best to remember what Davina showed her when she did an example of the dance with Quinn. Damien and Nevaeh walked around one another; their hands interlocked as they did so. A playful smirk played on Damien's lips as he pushed her out and twirled her back into his embrace. Her back to his, the memory of last night fresh in her memory as goosebumps erupted on her skin at the thought. She pulled away to finish the last part of the routine, facing him before holding out her hand which he took carefully before leaning down to pepper a sweet kiss upon the top of her hand. Nevaeh's chest rose and fell quickly from the dance or just from this action, she wasn't sure. Damien slowly looked up, looking at her through his dark lashes as he released her hand and stood tall. He smoothed out his hair and placed his hands in his pocket as he turned to look at Davina and Medici.

"So, all good?"

The two stood still, their jaws open in shock as Medici was the first to break the silence.

"Yes?"

"Great. Cut her some slack then, yeah?" He looks over at a seemingly stunned Nevaeh before winking at her, his lips curling up in a devilish smirk as he starts to walk toward the bench Quinn sat on to retrieve his suit jacket.

"Make sure she gets to Lennox before two so he can have time prepping her gown for the ball. I need her to be done with her itinerary by five."

"Why five?" Nevaeh finally speaks up, her voice holding an edge of curiosity as he looks over his shoulder at her.

"I'll be done with my meetings by six. If you're done an hour before me, you'll have time to get ready for dinner. You must eat."

"I can always eat later if anyone needs extra time to work. I hate rushing anyone—"

"—well, you aren't, I am because I want to have dinner with you at a decent hour."

Nevaeh blushed significantly at his words, her hands folding together in front of her as she cleared her throat.

"Is that alright with you?" He asks sarcastically, his eyes looking her over with a playfulness which seemed familiar to her.

"Maybe." She blurted, her eyes widening ever so slightly at her boldness which he only whistled to in response.

He mumbled a daft but humorous "alright" and walked out of the ballroom without another word.

She looked over at Davina, who rushed over with a smile and squeal.

"I swear to Leviathan, you have him wrapped around your finger."

The Renegade Division's land was made up of a ragtag group of sinister and unforgiving damned. They lived in a town of ruin which didn't bother them at all, their territory marked by bloodied stakes with their enemies or traitors' heads attached. They occupied no more than 160 acres of land, surrounded by darkness and the haunted forest to keep them somewhat hidden from the opposing divisions. Their leader, Morana Lenoir, daughter of Division two's late leaders Daemon and Etienne Lenoir. They were once fair rulers but turned ruthless once Danica's War occurred. Daemon, once very close friends with Leviathan, was forced to turn against him in wake of Danica's death due to Leviathan's torturous reign.

Morana was both smart and beautiful, two very dangerous attributes she used to her advantage. Riddled with her parent's death, she made it her life's work to avenge them and bring back the old order of Hell in all its unyielding righteousness. Her long, sleek black hair cascaded down her back like a silken black curtain. Her eyes were a blank, icy blue, framed with dark lashes. Her face was angular yet extensively feminine, her plump pink lips and perfectly pointed nose fit her features in a dark yet aesthetically pleasing way. She sat upon a mess of melted steel and armor; a frightening up-cycled throne made from her loyal followers. Her right hand, Miako Himura, described as a soulless mercenary, stood tall beside her throne in wait.

Morana's throughs were cut short when one of her followers came running into the chamber.

"M'lady! Excuse my haste, though I have reason."

Morana, unwavering, looked down at him in a mix of annoyance and somewhat disgust.

"What?" She spat pointedly as the man rose from his knees before her.

"We've received word from the palace. A gift. It's marked with your name."

This caused Morana to stand, the man stepping back a few times as she ascended the small steps of the throne to floor level. Miako stepped quietly and smoothly behind her until she stopped on the steps.

"Then bring it. NOW!" she exclaimed loudly; her eyes wide as she watched him trip away as he ran. She looked back at Miako, causing her to nod once in understanding before she looked forward again with a roll of her eyes. She knew something was off and Miako was ready for the bloodshed which might come of it. In a minute, a group of her men entered again, this time carrying what looked like a large rectangle box with handles all around. It was wrapped tightly in black silk ribbon, tied tightly at the top with a perfect bow. Morana tightened her fists at the sight of it, leveling her eyes as they sat down on the floor with a chilling crack. She slowly looked up to her men, then back down to the perfectly ribboned box before speaking.

"Open it," she stated, merely above a whisper, as her men looked around at one another expectedly.

"I said, OPEN IT!" she shouted then, making them rush into action as they all clawed away at the ribbon before stopping at the sight of a red envelope with black writing on its center. Morana stepped forward, ripping the parcel from the center of the box before handing it to Miako to open. She steps down so she stands beside her now, opening the pristine red envelope with focus as she removes a crisp written letter.

"Read it—out loud." She instructs, causing Miako to follow her instruction in a second.

Miako clears her throat, beginning to walk out into Morana's line of sight.

"This message is for Morana of the newfound Renegade Division in the south. You have done little to nothing before now to deserve any harsh treatment or punishment from the crown, though your actions have now proven otherwise. Your merciless leadership style could have proven much value to the royal guard, yet your obstinacy has ruined any chance of that ever occurring. I wish you had chosen another path in terms of leadership, as now you have created a solid point in where you stand with the crown. Your teachings and leadership have infected the realms division's, which has caused a mass of chaos and uprising in its wake. One of your followers dared to sit at my table, in my kingdom, and disrespect my authority and soon-to-be-Queen—" Miako stopped then, her eyes flitting upward to meet a now stunned Morana, who walked up to Miako with ferocity.

"His who?" She seethed lowly, her lips quivering in anger as Miako didn't react. She continued reading,

"—I hope that this will help you guide your decision for whatever you may be hoping to accomplish. As you know, I do not tolerate insubordination or insults of any kind regarding the crown and this realm. Any force against me, you'll receive it much worse in contrast. Your attempts to undermine my rule are juvenile as is your personal belief in what you think is right for this realm. I hope this gift will kick you back to reality, where you realize that you are the subject who respects their ruler who, in fact, allows you to breathe where you stand. If you have any questions or concerns regarding this letter and where it leaves you in this realm, I'm sure we can discuss it at the upcoming annual Blood Ball." Miako lowers the letter from eye level to look at a shaking Morana, her eyes nearly bloodshot from anger and trying her best not to cry.

"It's signed 'King Damien Blake'— "

"—open the fucking box!" She nearly roars, sending the men before her scrambling as they tried to open the nailed box with their bare hands. They succeeded in no time, with bloodied and splintered hands because of their prying.

The "gift" sent by the King was not at all welcoming or kind in any means—it was a heinous warning; one that left Morana seeing red. Inside the box, now open on full display, was a dead and nearly unrecognizable Rick. One of her most trusted informants, now dead in a box from the King himself. She screamed in pure anger, cursing his name as the men before her immediately got down on their knees and bowed before her to spare them of her wrath.

"I want him to suffer—he will know pain and suffering more than any damned soul he processes. He wants a war. I'll give him one he won't recover from."

CHAPTER 19

CARNIVAL OF THE ANIMALS

Nevaeh was focused, her eyes scanning the text of the worn book she held in her hands. She sighed softly, turning the page as she knitted her brows together slightly in what seemed to be curiosity. Lennox looked at her from time to time in between his measuring and pinning.

"Len?" She called expectedly then, causing the man to turn in her direction.

"Yes?"

"Earth has nearly seven billion inhabitants. Does that seem accurate or a bit absurd?"

"Absurd? I don't think so. Earth is quite massive. I remember my time there well, even if it was so long ago."

Nevaeh looked up then, her eyes raking over Lennox as he continued to fidget with the scarlet red fabric of her gown on its mannequin bodice.

"Your time? As in, you've been to Earth?"

"Honey, I'm from Earth."

"Why didn't you tell me?" she asks exasperatedly, slamming the book shut as her eyes went wide with wonder. She slowly made her way closer to Lennox, her eyes almost cartoon-like as she ogled at the man before her.

"What's there to tell? It's the past, I live here now. Besides, when could I have even brought that up in conversation and not be weird?"

"Oh, I don't know, maybe when you see me with my head between a book's spine regarding Earth?" She replied sarcastically, earning a curt chuckle from Lennox. He gives her a sly look before pinning a part of the dress, allowing the silence to envelope them.

"You're not getting out of this Lennox. Tell me everything you know. How long ago was this?"

He sighs in contempt, stopping his nimble movements on the fabric before carefully smoothing some fine lines in the silk. Neveah immediately picks up on his hesitation, her eyelids fluttering briefly as she parted her lips to speak.

"Was it bad?"

Lennox gave her a reassuring half smile, motioning her to take a seat on the small steps of the fashion stage before sitting beside her.

"I…I miss the sun. Sunshine," he says calmly, his tone soft as he seemed to reminisce in the moment. "I was a morning person, I loved to wake up early just to watch the sun rise and peak above the high-rise…" He looked over to Neveah as she watched him in anticipation, her brows slightly tugged together in concern. He sighs, clearing his throat as he looks towards the unfinished gown. He saw it completely made up, as he usually does, making the half-done hanging fabric comical to him.

"You do know that you must do something horrible or do a multitude of bad things to end up here. You don't just choose to come to Hell or even go to Heaven. A lot of people say it's complicated, but it really isn't, it's quite black and white to me." He says almost breathlessly, Neveah reaching out and carefully placing her hand on his forearm in comfort. He smiles at the action, his eyes brimming with tears as Neveah squeezed his arm softly.

"I used to design when I lived on Earth too. I loved to create; the essence of making something from absolutely nothing fascinated me in a way I don't think I can ever explain. I designed dresses and suits and shoes and handbags for the most important of them all—"

Nevaeh drew in a breath in anticipation, her eyes lighting up for a moment before he continued.

"—me."

Neveah tilted her head for a moment, causing Lennox to laugh genuinely at her confusion.

"You?"

"Yeah. I designed for myself, for a very long time. I dressed friends along the way as well, but I never garnered any fame from my craft. It wasn't right for people like me to make clothes and profit from it at the time."

"People like you?" she asked carefully, Lennox closing his eyes as he hummed in acknowledgement.

"People like me, people who chose to follow their heart and love someone who looks like them."

Nevaeh's face contorted for a moment before she froze.

"You're…"

"—I honestly thought it was obvious. I mean, this much fashion sense doesn't come from a man who flies straight sweetheart, trust me."

Nevaeh laughs lightly, leaning in to get Lennox to keep talking.

"I thought I had it all figured out, you know? I was in love, he was everything I wished for, everything I wanted, he checked off every box on my list; it was magical for sure. Then, in a minute it just—" He snaps his fingers to emphasis his statement. "—turned into a nightmare." He sniffled, Neveah sitting back slightly to give him space as she looked down at the plum carpet beneath them.

"Pierre was charming, and he knew how to get in your head without doing too much. He knew everything I ever wanted and more because I opened my heart and allowed it to bleed all over him until he became my deepest desire. He knew what to say, how to say it…I hurt a lot of people taking his side. I should've known. Though, when you're in love with someone…you're blinded. You can't think straight. It's both frightening and exciting."

"Len, you don't have to tell me—"

"—I was young, free, and had someone who believed in me. I swore I didn't need anything else besides that. I had no one else, no family or close friends to count on or pull my head from the clouds. Everything was picture perfect, a dream…until it wasn't. He…he took advantage of me; of that kind-free spirit." Lennox allowed tears to fall now, his blonde brows tugging together as he let a shaky breath release past his quivering lips.

"I felt empty, so hurt, so betrayed. A man I loved so desperately and fully; I never knew he could hurt me so badly. So, as I laid there, stripped, and broken, he left with everything I ever had or dreamed of. All my happiness, my meaning, my purpose on earth…it left with him. So…when you feel so down, so absolutely wrecked, you just want it to stop. You want the feeling to go away, you want the pain to cease so you could enjoy the sunshine again." Lennox croaks, his head shaking slightly as he tries to remain calm.

Neveah cried silently beside him; her tears steadily streamed down her freckled cheeks as Lennox wiped away at his hazel eyes.

"Next thing I knew, I woke up in a desolate land of ruin. Screams and blood and heat, it was everywhere…it consumed me. Later when I was being processed, Levi was running through my memories when he and Queen Danica made a mutual decision to give me a second chance at life. To continue the things that I wanted to achieve. It is something I can never repay them for, even if I tried."

"I can't even imagine how you could've felt. I'm so sorry Len." Neveah stated softly, grabbing his arm, and hugging him. She let her head rest on his shoulder as the two sat in a moment of silence.

"It's funny, you know, because I see a bit of my younger self in you." Lennox quipped suddenly, causing her to sit up and look at him expectedly.

"How do you mean?"

"You're determined, fearless, and stubborn as hell,"

"—I am not fearless,"

Lennox laughs heartily then, Nevaeh's lips threatening to turn upwards as he shook his head in amusement.

"Yet you say nothing of being determined and stubborn."

"I can't help it. I've always been this way."

"Never let it go. Hold on to that ferocity and passion. It will head you in your darkest moment. Just when you think you're down, you'll find quite the opposite in hindsight."

Nevaeh nodded once in understanding, standing up as she took Lennox's hand and forced him upright.

"It sounds like you've been spending too much time with Medici."

Lennox can't help the deep laugh that fell past his lips, his hands reaching for the silk of the gown once again like he never left.

"You think you're a jokester now, hm? Get back to your little book, why don't you?"

Nevaeh's room had been stockpiled with books from the time she arrived in Hell almost six months ago. She nearly complied a mini library in her room, with books ranging from wall to wall and almost to the ceiling in one corner of her extravagant quarters. She had meekly asked Damien for a little help with organization, which to her surprise, came nearly instantly. She had left her room one morning to do her daily routine and rehearsals with Davina only to come back to neatly stocked bookcases alongside the side wall of her room. A part of her thought it was rude to leave all the books in her room, as they should be returned to the library, though she would often get lazy and forget to switch out the texts when getting new ones to read.

This evening, the curly haired angel sat comfortably on the ledge of the main courtyard's fountain. She felt particularly content in the moment, the sound of the dark water spouting from its grandiose statue in the center was almost soothing as she read through an earth-ian text. She was in a world of her own, her senses occupied enough not to sense eyes watching her from afar. Davina watched on coolly, walking down the hall overlooking the courtyard with a small smirk on her face. She had a seemingly fun idea, but one that was nearly childish to bring up to a usually timid Nevaeh. The angel was very mellow and even tired in times like these, it was almost like she would breathe life into the books rested in her palms. Davina rounded the corner and began her decent of the stairs before quietly walking over to where Nevaeh rested peacefully.

"It's a bit late to be out reading, don't you think?"

Nevaeh's head jerked up, her eyes wide in surprise before they settled in recognition.

"Nighttime is the best time to read, for me at least."

Davina nodded once, looking her over once before turning her face to the darkening sky.

"I've an idea. It requires you to leave your book behind, though. Interested?"

Nevaeh cracks her book closed, her fingers a temporary bookmark as she then crossed her legs before Davina.

"It depends. What are you up to?"

Davina hums curtly, looking down at the cover of her book which makes her raise a brow. Nevaeh realizes this immediately, turning it over in her grasp before looking at Davina's intrigued expression.

"The Blood Ball is two days away. You've done a great job in preparing for it. I figured you'd want to relax."

Nevaeh stands then, her eyes squinted in curiosity as Davina tilted her head forward.

"I'm going to do this regardless of if you come, just thought I'd ask if you wanted to join me."

"Where?" Nevaeh asks rather flatly, only causing Davina's mischievousness to reach her eyes.

"Do you like the water?"

"I'm sorry?"

"Are you a fan of the water? Do you know how to swim?"

Nevaeh paled almost immediately, instant flashbacks of her falling from such a great height towards the blue ocean waves all those months ago…

"Are you okay?" Davina asks hurriedly, her hand reaching out but retracting almost immediately upon remembering what happened the last time she touched her.

Nevaeh sits back down on the stone ledge with a deep sigh, shaking her head slightly before giving Davina a reassuring nod.

"I'm okay, just got a little dizzy."

"Have you eaten? I could call for some food, have it sent to your room."

"No, that's unnecessary…and to answer your previous question, yes, I know how to swim."

Davina's face brightens almost instantly, her lips curving upward as she clasps her hands together.

"Perfect. I could call for something to be brought to the pavilion, then."

Almost thirty minutes later, Nevaeh found herself clad in a swimsuit alongside Davina. Her face held a permanent blush at the lack of clothing she wore, even with a sheer lace coverup. Davina, in contrast, was confident in her two-piece as she seemed to strut as she led the way to the water pavilion. The abstract building stood alone away from the castle, a glistening obsidian pathway leading up to its entrance. Nevaeh was at a loss for words upon seeing its architecture, the building resembling that of an unraveling spiraled sphere.

The building and walkway were surrounded by small patches of fire that helped light the way. Davina looked back in what seemed to be excitement as Nevaeh gave a small smirk in reply. The front doors were an opaque black, just light enough to see through to the other side. Davina pulled the doors open to a small space which had two sides of entry. She didn't stop walking, Nevaeh walking after her to the left before she stopped upon entering the vast opening of the pavilion. A large pool of black water lay untouched in front of her, as well as two smaller circular bodies of water on either side of the large pool. She looked up to take in the beautiful sky, now a dark navy littered with small specks of stars here and there. She smiled to herself, closing her eyes briefly as she took in the smell before her.

It was salty but sweet, a hint of smoke, and—her eyes opened in shock at the familiar scent. Her head turning slightly to her left, towards the back of the room. In the circular pool, the back of his shoulders facing her, was Damien. Nevaeh felt like she was going to be sick, her legs nearly giving out as her anxiety shot through the roof. She quickly looked over to Davina who seemed to be racing back towards her with a knowing look.

"I didn't know prissy pants were going to be here. I'm going to come back later—"

"—no, no, no, Davina don't leave me—"

Davina shushes her quietly, tilting her head towards Damien with a wink. Nevaeh looked as if she was going to be sick.

"I promise it's okay. He isn't going to bite. Well," She stops upon seeing Nevaeh's pale expression. "I'm joking, relax. Go take a dip. I'll see you in the morning."

"No, you can't do this to me." She seethes lowly but Davina only gives a pained smile before tip toeing away and into the darkness of the entryway they just came from. Nevaeh stood there frozen for a moment before she swallowed the lump in her throat. She fiddled with the satin ribbon of her cover-up as she carefully turned around toward the pool again. She breathed deeply, beginning to walk towards the back of the room towards a still Damien. She watched as he seemed to roll his bare shoulders, the small droplets of water which littered his skin seemed to give him a glow. She felt her face grow redder the closer she stepped, her hands trembling as she stopped a few feet from the circular pool.

Their last dinner went well, though there was a rising tension between them that neither of the two wanted to address. It sent Nevaeh into a fit of frustration and embarrassment, as it was a very newfound set of emotions she's never felt before. She desperately wanted Damien to kiss her, to see if he tasted like smoke and leather. The more she thought about these things, the more upset she would make herself if it didn't happen. Damien, in contrast, has been having the best self-control known to man. If it were anyone else, he would've jumped their bones and been onto the next seductress in sight. Though this was different, Damien reminded himself of this every time he caught her staring at him with a deep blush across her striking features.

She realized the steam coming from the water, the heat making her sweat even more than what she currently was. She tried to steady her breathing and focus on the rushing water around her before she inhaled a deep breath, making herself known as she cleared her throat expectedly.

"Would you like some company?"

Damien turned his head then, his side profile nearly making Nevaeh drop to her knees in defeat at how attractive he looked. His face was flushed slightly from the heat, his eyes gleaming and playful. He looked almost vulnerable and humane in this atmosphere. Almost human.

"Come in and find out for yourself." He replied casually, reaching back to stretch his arms along the smooth granite of the pool.

Nevaeh couldn't help herself, dropping down so she rested in a crouched position with her folded hands on her forehead. She was shaking, in fear or anticipation of what might happen—she couldn't think, let alone decide. She did decide at that moment though, that she wouldn't let him have the satisfaction of seeing her this flustered. She realized early on that he loved making her heart race, perfect for an egotistical king of hell. She stood and lifted her head high, undoing the satin ribbon of her cover-up as she spoke rather confidently.

"Close your eyes so I can get in the water, then."

Damien scoffed, water splashing softly as he tried to stifle a laugh.

"You're kidding me. You're in a swimsuit. Wait, you are in a—"

"—just shut up and close your eyes!" She nearly combusted, causing Damien to sigh in defeat and comply.

She carefully stepped forward and around Damien, stopping right before he could see her.

"Are you sure your eyes are closed?" she asks pointedly, causing him to hang his head back to reveal his eyes snapped shut.

"I'm pretty sure they are."

"Whatever." She grumbles, walking to the stairs leading into the water. She was a bit nervous, seeing the seemingly treacherous black water up close. She carefully stepped down, the heat of the water causing goosebumps to erupt all over her body. She continued forward until she was shoulder length in the water. She couldn't believe how deep the pool went and she was also curious to how Damien sat along the edge of the pool; his chest only half covered by the sinister looking water.

"You can open now." She stated.

Upon her words, Damien slowly opened his dark green eyes which now bored into Nevaeh's brown ones.

"You know, you're a little tease." He spoke casually, making Nevaeh tilt her head. She tried not to show how affected she was in the moment by his words, so she rolled her eyes before looking up at the ceiling. She smiled slightly, admiring the spiral structure and the stars that peeked through the glass. Damien leveled his eyes towards her, a certain glint in them which made goosebumps erupt all over Nevaeh's tan skin once more.

"I don't know what you're talking about. I think you're getting a little light-headed from the all the heat."

He bares his teeth as he smiles, a hearty chuckle rippling through the water between them as he licks his lips. His teeth claimed his bottom lip as he revels in the silence between them, his eyes greedily taking in this new version of Nevaeh before him. She tried her hardest not to look at him, instead wading around as she admired the inside of the pavilion.

"Your heart is about to jump out of your chest." Damien states quietly and rather smugly as she stops for a moment, taking a deep breath before standing up straight near the stairs.

"Thank you for stating the obvious. I'd have you know I'm not much of a fan of water."

"Then why come to the pavilion?"

Nevaeh stopped then, turning to face him as he tilted his head.

She squinted her eyes and went to answer before closing her mouth in defeat. He was right. Her once confident façade began crumbling faster than she could've anticipated.

Damien pushed himself off the ledge of the pool, slowly creeping towards a frozen Nevaeh. In her anxiety-filled state, she pushed her arm out to stop him from coming closer to her. Before she could process what was happening, her palm lay flat on his toned torso, her eyes settling upon a few spots of ink branded into his skin. Where she was once wading in the water, he stood strong. The height difference was clear and almost comical now.

"Like I said…tease." He stated smugly, grabbing her by her wrist and removing her palm from his skin with a smirk.

"You have tattoos." She began deeply, trying to change the topic immediately to take the spotlight off her faltering emotions. Damien searched her eyes as he answered her rather softly.

"I do. I have quite a few, actually. What do you think?"

"Well, I was never allowed any. They're known as a physical sin in Heaven; *to tarnish your skin with ink is to tarnish your love of he who bled for it.*"

He scoffs, walking past her a bit so more of his arms are visible above the water. His hand reaches over to point to his left triceps where a group of letters lay inked.

"These are my mother's initials,"

He reveals his forearms from under the dark water, each marked with two slender upside-down crosses. The sight makes Nevaeh's eyes pop from her head, making her lower his arms with her hands so they were under the water again and out of sight.

"What? Does that bother you?" He asks jokingly, his voice muddled with laughter as he tried his hardest to hold back his spreading smile.

"Well, yeah. I was taught that…that type of cross is just pure evil, and you have *two.*"

"Well, yeah, I'm kind of evil personified. I thought you'd be accustomed to that by now." He responds mockingly, tilting his head slightly as she glares at him.

"Don't patronize me."

He rolls his eyes, making her stand a bit straighter in contrast to his comfortable demeanor. Damien couldn't help the double take he took. Nevaeh immediately notices, splashing him harshly as she sunk deeper into the water with a scowl.

"God, you're a pervert! You didn't even try to hide it—"

"—I'm sorry to burst your bubble princess but I was looking at your mark."

Nevaeh softened a bit there, looking him over for any trace of deceit but she found none in his emerald-green eyes. She sighed, standing again so her mark was clearly visible again. Damien got a closer look, his thumb grazing over the branded skin of her chest softly before catching sight of her eyes.

"I have it, too, you know."

Her eyes widened, splashing a bit in shock.

"What? Where? Since when?"

He gave a mischievous smirk before walking past her and towards the stairs. She watched in a mix of confusion and anticipation. She admired how the water rolled off his toned back and muscular arms, his dark hair dribbling dark water drops down his spine as he then stopped at the middle of the stairs. He turned and began to pull his swim shorts a bit down before Nevaeh shouted in protest.

"OH MY GOD—WHAT ARE YOU DOING?!" She smacked her face in the process of covering her eyes, her face turning beet red at the action.

Damien stopped, his shoulders dropping as he gave her a disappointed and annoyed look.

"Relax, little saint." He teases, his turn to roll his eyes.

She peaks through her fingers to see Damien's brandished mark on the lower half of his hip. Her jaw drops slightly.

"Wow…that's…have you always had this?"

"Mhm. Since I was born. Its more like a birth mark to me, though."

"That's so interesting. I got mine when I fell through the portal. Does it ever hurt? Mine feels a little sore from time to time."

"No, it doesn't ever bother me."

He descended back down into the water, pushing himself closer as Nevaeh pushed herself backward to keep distance between them. The pool dipped significantly under her as she stepped backward, causing her to go under the water for a second only to be pushed upward by strong hands. Nevaeh stilled immediately, Damien's strong grip nearly zapping her into another dimension. He stared at her mischievously, her cheeks red from the action and from the heat of the water around them.

"You're not a strong swimmer, are you?"

"Like I said, not the biggest fan of water." She replied shakily, making him slowly pull her towards the deep end where she first found him.

"Well, this isn't the smartest place to be. Thankfully I'm here to keep you from drowning."

He places her down on the ledge to sit, her arms immediately going to grip the ledge of the pool for balance. He sits beside her and watches her as she settles in. He could tell she was nervous, from the depth of the water or the proximity of their nearly naked bodies—he wasn't sure.

"I'll chew Davina's ear off when I see her. Can't believe she left a weak swimmer all by themselves."

Nevaeh chuckles briefly, shaking her head slightly.

"Yeah, I'm starting to think Davina knew what she was doing." she says sheepishly, avoiding his eyes as she looked up at the spiraling night sky.

"Yeah." He chuckled lowly, looking forward. He then looked at her again, letting the silence envelope them for a moment before his brows furrowed in thought.

"May I ask you something? Seriously, though."

Nevaeh looks at him, her face kind of falling at the deep shift in emotion.

"Surely."

He seems to swallow his words for a moment before shifting his body to face hers more straight-on.

"I know you aren't from Hell, and it must be very diffi-cult for you to acclimate your time and by extension your life here…though a part of me really longs to know if you're actually happy."

Nevaeh freezes, her mouth dry as she opens her mouth to speak but no words follow. Damien noticed and immediately tenses, his once playful features turning defensive and even confused at her reaction. He turns forward and sits still even in the ebbing water. Nevaeh's heart rate increases steadily at his change in demeanor before she finally finds the right words.

"I can say that I've been treated rather kindly during my stay so far…that is something I would've never imagined would happen as a visitor of Hell."

"A visitor? That's what you think of yourself? A visitor who has an itinerary and time slot to leave. So, like, this is a vacation for you? Just a pit stop until you get to your destination—"

"—Damien, I never said that. I'm just saying—"

"—you do know you're bound to this realm, right? You can't leave, even if you wanted to."

Nevaeh became defensive at his statement and harsh tone, her answer coming without thought.

"I can leave when I'm willing and ready to. What will happen? You can't stop me from going where I please. I'm not bound to anything unless I, myself claim to be—no realm or ruler will dictate how I choose to live my life."

"So why are you here if you're so unhappy, hm? Why continue to stay and make yourself miserable? Why continue to stay?"

"I never said I was miserable, Damien. Never did I once say that…why are suddenly being so abrasive?"

"You didn't answer my question." Damien spat, pushing himself around and up, so he was out of the pool. Nevaeh watched in a mix of horror and sadness as he nearly stormed away from her.

"Damien! Don't walk away from me like that! Hey, I'm talking to you!" She shouted in frustration, following his same movements until she was on dry land once more. She quickly grabbed her cover up and pulled it over her wet body while pushing her slippers on before quickly rushing after Damien who had just left her line of sight. She could hear her heartbeat in her ears, she could feel the blood pooling there in embarrassment too as she chased after the King of Hell. Anyone in their right mind would run in the opposite direction of an angry king, yet Nevaeh found herself nearly sprinting to match his long strides. She pushed open the pavilion doors, planting her feet as she watched Damien walk down the obsidian walkway towards the castle. She didn't think twice before speaking.

"You really know how to ruin a good time don't you?" She spat loudly, causing him to halt in his tracks. She watched, chest heaving, as the muscles in his back tensed at her words. He turned around, his face void of any kind of playfulness or warmth she had witnessed in the pavilion.

"Me? It's *you*. You're the one who knows how to fuck up a good time. Here I am, being so kind and open to someone who couldn't care less about me and my feelings. I knew this wouldn't work from the start. I told Medici that. I said this wouldn't end well but he told me to try. So, to please everyone else and be the bigger person, here I was, trying, and yet, here you are at the end of it all! — still a selfish bitch!"

Nevaeh gasped lowly, her jaw falling slack at his venomous words before she quickly walks up to him. She pushed him forcefully backward only to have him stagger a step backwards.

"How dare you say something like that to me?! Blame me for your insecurities? I'm a selfish bitch? The only reason you've been nice to me is because you have no other choice! You said it for yourself! You're only acting on the precipice of a hundred-year-old prophecy that claims I'm stuck here for the rest of my life, so you're trying to make this place seem likable but guess what, Damien? It's NOT! I'm not accustomed to this type of life! No matter how hard I try, I'm missing home more than I ever thought I would. I'd rather jump off another cliff than stand here and take misguided insults from someone who can't maturely express their emotions but rather throw childish insults instead!" She shouts, her pointer finger digging into his chest before he grabs her wrist forcefully and shoves it aside.

"You want to know something? You're right. I was childish to let my guard down and try to be a different person for someone who couldn't give a fuck in the first place. So, here's my honest apology, princess. I'm sorry for not showing you the real me that everyone knows. The real me that makes everyone's skin crawl, the real me that fills them with terror when they hear my name. You're so miserable, huh? What a horrible and miserable situation to be in, oh, to be waited on hand and fucking foot twenty-four hours in a day. Listen, how about I just make

Medici open a portal for your ungrateful ass to leave and never return? Because guess what, after today, I'm done being Mr. Nice Guy!"

"You don't have to ask him anything because I'll ask him myself!" She screams back at him, tears falling freely as he tries to remain unfazed by them.

"You don't have the jurisdiction to make those kinds of demands here." He spits sinisterly.

"Oh, you're such a big man, Damien. Go ahead and tell me how insignificant I am here compared to you, like I don't already know. You think you scare me? Newsflash, you don't."

Damien blanks, his mind going dark in a second as he goes to grab her face but stops right before making contact. His hands shake on either side of her head before he retreats, placing them on top of his head as he walked backward to give them a large amount of space between them.

"You haven't seen scary, Nevaeh. You haven't even scratched the fucking surface." He seethed, his chest rising and falling rapidly as he tried to calm down his breathing.

Nevaeh is choking back sobs, her body weak from fighting the urge of crying and screaming as she places the rest of her energy into reaching upwards towards the necklace around her neck. She grabbed the emerald pendant, her knuckles turning white from the grip before yanking it strongly as he looked on in pure horror. Damien couldn't believe he let himself go, how he allowed himself to say such spiteful things to the woman he loved. Yes, the woman he loved.

As soon as the thought passed his mind, she pushed past him, throwing the necklace at his feet. As she passed, he tried reaching out only to miss her by inches. He let his arm fall, his chest heaving as he stood in place and tried to navigate what had just happened. He stood in place for a moment, Nevaeh long gone, before he seethed from pain. He groaned in anguish, his hands claiming the area of his hip before crashing to the ground. The searing sensation made him see stars, his fingers claiming the wet fabric of his shorts and tugging them down furiously to see an alarming sight. His birthmark, the one that never hurt him or bothered him once before, was now inflamed and branded red. It was like someone cut over the outline of the mark. He gasped for air; his eyes glassy as he fought back the pain. He didn't know what was occurring or why. The only thing he could think of was Nevaeh.

The angel made it back to her room, her body collapsing as she closed the door behind her. Her hand claimed the marked skin over her heart, a small prickling sensation enough for her to rub the skin to soothe it. It didn't last long, her vision claiming the bed in front of her with longing before she decided the floor was a better option. She laid there motionless, her body hiccupping from her vicious crying fit before it ceased completely with her finally finding sleep.

CHAPTER 20

HEADS WILL ROLL

"You're very tense, love. Is everything alright? You haven't said a word since you stepped up here." Lennox playfully stated as his nimble fingers carefully grazed Nevaeh's rib cage to smooth over some ruffled silk. He gave a reassuring smile, Nevaeh trying but failing to match his. She instead looked straight forward at the golden architecture of the studio doors as Lennox continued to do his last-minute finishing touches on her gown. Lennox did not like how she was acting; he knew immediately something was off when he collected her from her room this morning.

"You know, you can talk to me. I won't utter a word to anyone, not even that old bag, Medici."

Nevaeh closes her eyes briefly, allowing a sigh to escape her lips as she looked over to Lennox.

"It doesn't matter how I feel. It won't change what happened."

"What is it that happened?" he asked briskly, not missing a beat as the fallen angel shook her head in distaste.

"No, I don't want you to get involved. If you were to get in trouble because of me, I wouldn't ever forgive myself. I'll be alright."

"Nevaeh, don't you go worrying about me. What is it that has made you like this? I can't bear the sight of you this upset."

Nevaeh grabs his hands, squeezing them gently in reassurance before releasing them and standing up straight once more.

"It doesn't matter, really. I just have to get through this evening in one piece and then we can discuss it. I can't unpack it all right now. So, let us just focus on this, okay?" She says deeply, placing her hands on either side of her body to accentuate the almost complete dress.

Lennox sighs softly, nodding once as he went back to adjusting the fabric. She caught a glimpse of herself in a side view mirror on the wall to the right of her, her face pale beside the flush of blush across her cheeks. She blinked away the tears that threatened to spill over, her stomach in complete knots over the evening she had ahead of her. She had not seen Damien in two days, their last meeting explosive to say the least. She did not want to think about how awkward tonight would be following that evening outside of the water pavilion. She had prayed it would be rather cool, that the two of them would just play their respected roles and part amicably at the end of the night. She knew deep down that would not happen, that she was being too naïve and childish even in her thought process. Damien was enraged, she had never seen him so angry. She knew he would not live that down, especially after what was said between them.

Nevaeh took a deep breath, realizing she harbored pent-up tension in her shoulders and chest as she suddenly smiled at the large full body mirror a few feet in front of her.

What a perfect smile, a perfect façade.

"Is something the matter, Damien? You seem rather preoccupied this evening." Medici asked genuinely to a rather stoic looking Damien as he adjusted his ruby stone cufflinks in the full-length mirror before him. One of Lennox's aides dusted his shoulders briskly and tended to his shirt collar before bowing before him and exiting. Medici stood by idly, his hands crossed in front of him as he studied the man silently.

"I'm fine, what makes you assume I'm not?"

"I think you forgot that I'm lightyears older than you, and that I basically raised you. I can tell when there's a war happening up there." He states casually, his finger claiming his temple before walking towards Damien and clearing his throat.

"Call me old-fashioned but, I don't think its smart to go into a party with a loaded heart, hm? A lot can happen if its punctured."

"Like?"

"You'll suffocate in your own blood for one—and the blood that sprays? Those are the words you wish you didn't say but did anyway. Others will likely be in the vicinity of said spray, to make matters worse."

"Well, I'm already exsanguinated. So, what's the worst that could happen?" He replies monotonously, smoothing the lapels of his suit jacket before blinking twice at his reflection. Medici looks down, words failing as his lips formed a solid line at Damien's rather glum mood on such a celebratory evening. It was unlike him as of late. It worried Medici. Damien was starting to act like his old self, the ruthless and cold being everyone despised. Medici looked him over carefully, his eyes raking over the King's dark features before his deep voice broke the silence.

"I'm ready." He started rather coldly, walking out of his room as Medici followed slowly. His guards followed suit; the faceless beings who were decked out in black attire from head to toe was a frightening sight to behold. The stygian guard was also on standby just in case things went awry at any point during the highly exciting evening. Damien sighed heavily, blinking rather slowly as he stopped in front of the door to Lennox's studio. He bit his tongue, his jaw jutted ever so slightly in a mix of anger and frustration of what lied behind the gold doors. He could already feel her racing heart, her stomach which was tied in an abundance of knots. Nevaeh felt him too, her heart almost stopping for a moment as she placed her hands on her stomach in an almost bracing manner. Nevaeh was no longer wearing her bond protector—she threw her necklace in Damien's face two days ago. The action was childish above all, as all it did was heighten the duo's emotion and make it worse to bear. Her breath hitched, mirroring Damien's before he opened the doors with ferocity.

The king entered without warning. He was met with Nevaeh's nearly bare back, with Lennox smoothing out her waistline bodice. His golden eyes became frantic as he immediately walked around Nevaeh to zip up a quarter length of her dress. He then turned, bowing his head briefly before greeting the king formally.

"Good evening, My King."

"Lennox." He replied flatly, his eyes cascading down Nevaeh's backside for a millisecond before she turned around rather gracefully to meet his stern eyes.

They stared at one another for a moment, neither one of them uttering a word before Damien took charge.

"Let's go then."

Nevaeh didn't look at Lennox as she exited the room behind Damien, walking a good foot away from him as they ventured down the grand hallways of the castle to the main hall where guests were already filtering through castle security. Before they were to enter the ballroom, Damien stopped briskly and turned to face a rather surprised Nevaeh. She managed to stop awkwardly mid step to look up at him.

"This may not be good timing under the circumstances but, might I ask one favor of you this evening?"

Nevaeh nodded once, her breathing becoming shallow as she awaited his question. He dipped his head low, enough so he could whisper into her ear,

"In keeping up with appearances, could you at least act like you're happy here, just for the evening?"

He pulled back; his face serious as she did her best to fight back the oncoming tears. Her lips quivered at his statement, the previous night they spent with one another rushing back in waves as she managed to nod slightly in understanding. He looked her over once, his mouth opening to protest her submissive response before he closed it willfully.

"Good." He spat, taking her by the waist as the pair walked into the room smoothly. Nevaeh could feel her heartbeat in her ears as she tried to calm her anxiety which was through the roof. She did her best to blink back her tears, but one fell, making her wipe away at it briskly as she mustered up a small smile instead. A thousand eyes began to place themselves on her and Damien, a walkway being made for them as they careened themselves through the sea of bodies towards the high seated table at the far side of the room. The long table seemed to be suspended in the air, placed upon a morbid but spectacular monument of screaming damned etched into stone. Onyx spiraled stairs lead upwards to the table where Davina and Dante already sat expectedly. Damien stopped at the stairs, motioning for her to ascend before he followed her carefully. His guards then stood tall, blocking the stair entrance following Medici's ascent.

Damien sat on an all-black throne, the back of the seat sleek and spiked upwards. It looked almost Gothically modern, despite the grandiose Victorian style theme of the ball. Nevaeh took her place beside him, her seat almost identical to his but shorter in height. Medici sat on the other side of Damien with Dante as Davina sat beside her with an empty seat to Davina's right. She wanted to ask who it was for, but she decided against it in the defeating silence of the table. Everyone could feel the tension seeping into the air, averting their attention to their glasses before them or down at the eclectic group of hellions which occupied the room.

"Are you alright, Nevaeh?" Davina suddenly asks softly, her hand claiming the spot on the table in front of the angel. She nods softly in reply, giving a small smile and thinking swiftly on her feet.

"I'm just a bit nervous, is all. I'm feeling a little out of place."

Davina gives an encouraging smile as she looks out into the overflowing crowd.

"No need to be nervous. You've got hundreds of heads down there shaking at the sight of this entire table. You look like a Queen, already. No need to feel out of place."

Nevaeh gave a trying smile in reply, her eyes flitting outwards to the vast room and towards the entrance where well-dressed patrons continued to enter. Her sight was then taken from the far side of the room to the stairs below her. Her eyes lit up at the sight of a familiar face, her heart jumping excitedly at the sight of Lennox being escorted up by a member of the royal guard. Nevaeh's eyes widened as she pushed her seat back in attempts to get up but stopped abruptly when she met Lennox's eyes—something of a cautious warning to stay in her seat. He greets everyone politely with a curt bow and smile before taking the empty seat beside Davina. She casually pushed her chair forward again, looking over to Lennox with relief as he gave her a small smile.

"It seems I made it just in time." He commented casually, as she followed his gaze to the guards closing the large golden doors to the hall.

The lights seemed to dim just a bit, giving the room a cozy yet ominous feel which left Nevaeh feeling uneasy. She looked over to Damien now, his face hardened as he took hold of his cup and stood. Nevaeh became nervous, unsure if she should follow his suit or not. She decided against standing, which ultimately helped in her favor with Damien's short temper this evening. She didn't want to cause a scene in front of all these strangers. He cleared his throat, the piano ceasing to play as the people below turned to look up towards their daunting king. Damien's eyes raked over the audience a few times in silence, making note of familiar faces and ones he's never seen before. He raised his dark chalice in the air, a small smirk appearing on his lips as he began his long-awaited speech.

"My loyal subjects, I thank you all for attending this year's annual Blood Ball. I know this evening is not usually meant for formalities, but there are things happening in the realm that need to be addressed. I am sure you all are aware of the renegade division and their rise in sedition. I stand before you, assuring you that these individuals acting against the crown will be taken care of. Any act of treason against this realm's leadership will result in the upmost form of punishment. I am working tirelessly to ensure that Hell's laws and traditions remain intact and unspoiled by traitors and their treachery. There is no room for deceit among any of these realm's divisions nor on royal ground. I will be transparent with you all tonight. I have let you all down by allowing this group to become as well-rounded as we see them today. Though rest assure, it will not last long. Order among the divisions will be restored."

A round of applause ensues through the crowd as Damien nods in acknowledgement. After a moment, he parts his lips to speak but nothing follows. He swallows his words, his brows tugging together a bit in what seemed like conflicting emotion before he steals a side glance at a timid looking Nevaeh. He blinks a few times, shaking his head slightly as he allows a smirk to place itself on his lips as he addresses the people once again.

"I also would like to discuss a rumor that I am certain has been circulating from division to division regarding my personal relationship with…well the lovely woman sitting beside me tonight," he said, turning a bit and giving Nevaeh that smug look she knew so well before placing his hand out for her to take. She carefully stood from her seat, claiming his calloused hand before looking out into the stunned and whispering crowd.

"I would like to formally introduce to you, Nevaeh Azrael, your potential Queen of Hell, if she so willfully accepts."

Damien then places a chaste kiss upon the top of her hand, the intense blush flooding her cheeks unmissable as Damien released her hand in an instant. The gasps and hushed whispers that filled the hall and that kiss left Nevaeh feeling lightheaded even in the dimly lit room.

"Now, with business aside, it's time to enjoy tonight's festivities. A big thank you to Oz for being the magic behind the keys this evening. Also, to my right-hand man, the one who keeps me upright and on a straight path—well, as straight a path as a king of hell can follow—the irreplaceable Medici. I'd be rendered powerless without you." He raises his cup towards Medici, who tries to hide his pride as he nodded his head with a small smile.

"Enjoy the night, may every sin you make be worth your while." He raises his cup one last time, before downing the rest of the dark liquor in one gulp.

The music ensues as does the chatter and dancing, Damien taking his seat beside Nevaeh once again as she tries to remain calm. Her eyes began to water as all she could focus on was the laughter below, as she desperately hoped it wasn't geared towards her.

"Excuse me," she muttered meekly, her chair scraping against the marble as the patrons of the table stilled as they watched her go. Damien remained seated and looking forward. Medici sighed, straightening up and leaning over to him.

"You must stop whatever quarrel this is. It's not good for the elites to see their royals in disparage at such a joyful event. It's bad press,"

"—since when have you ever cared about press?"

"Since now, a few minutes ago, actually, when you announced that the realm would be bestowed a queen who hasn't uttered a word to you since we entered the hall."

"I'll handle it."

"I know you will, I am just worried with how you'll do it. Women are special creatures, Damien. Once you've done damage, it's easy to continue to inflict that damage rather than repair it."

"I know what to do. Just buy me some time while I do what I need to, alright? Davina," he turns.

to his sister who gives him an annoyed glare.

"I need you to keep an eye out for Morana. If she enters and Dante and I miss her by chance, she can cause trouble. Keep her busy and distracted."

"Why are you still sitting here blabbering on about something that hasn't even happened?"

Damien rolls his eyes, standing to leave before she grabs his wrist for him to stop.

"I know it may be hard for you, but some compassion would suffice in your situation."

Damien snatches his wrist from her grasp, Dante hot on his heels as the duo casually begin walking down the stairs and into the crowd. Damien is immediately met with elites who begin shaking his hand and attempting to spark conversation. He did his best to keep the interactions short and sweet, walking through the bodies towards the side door leading to the west wing.

"Your majesty, I must say, you put on a grand party. When will we be able to shake hands with your heavenly bride to be?" One elite stated rather boldly, as he shakes his hand vigorously. Damien looks at him warily, logging his face into his memory bank as does Dante before he gives a fake smile.

"Hopefully soon. She's quite a shy one. Excuse me,"

Damien gets through to the doors with the help of Dante, Damien focused as he began his walk through the hall. He sighed in frustration; his heart rate increasing by the second as he continued to search for Nevaeh. The pair finally rounded the corner to the library, though they entered complete silence. Damien stood in the center of the room and looked around, everything looking in pristine shape. He turned swiftly and exited the library and bee-lined for her room. He knocked feverishly at the gold-plated door, his knuckles becoming red from the force against the gold.

"Nevaeh? Are you in there?"

He continued to knock with no answer, his hands claiming the knob as Dante's eyes widened at the action.

"I'm coming in." He stated loudly, the door swinging open to an empty room. Again, everything was neat and in place. Her scent immediately hit him, the fragrant notes of vanilla and a hint of gardenia. It was as if she stood in front of him in the empty quarters of her room.

"I know where she is. She must be there."

CHAPTER 21

UNDERTOW

DAMIEN AND DANTE MADE their way outside to the main castle grounds, the stars in the deep navy sky were so intensely bright tonight. It was odd for stars to even appear in Hell, though they have been littering the night sky as of late. Damien makes his descent down the court stairs towards the garden. The whole scene gave him intense Déjà vu as it did Dante. His army general gave him a familiar look and nod before Damien turned and continued forward without him.

Nevaeh was indeed in the garden, sitting in the grass overlooking the hedge of the city on fire below her. The vibrant mix of fiery red and orange meddled with the ashen colors of black and charcoal gray was picturesque against the navy-blue sky above. It was as if the city were a blinking time bomb; the intense flashing of color enough to take someone's breath away.

The King of Hell stopped abruptly at the entrance of the garden hideaway, his slender frame reminiscent of one of his own stygian guards against the darkness of the night and dense hedge. He continued forward warily, the distant sounds of the city and party mixed with the steady crackling of fire up ahead made him somewhat uneasy. His silent footsteps carried him across the onyx pathway towards the cozy gazebo in the center of the small hideaway. He walked around it, his eyes finally landing on the angel who sat in the grass overlooking the fiery city before them. He placed his hands in his pockets, watching her for a moment before looking out into the chaos himself.

"It's quite the view, isn't it?"

Nevaeh doesn't turn to answer, her glossy eyes focused ahead of her as she responds.

"A view, yes."

Damien bites down on his tongue, trying his best not to let his anger get the best of him following her rather cold response.

"Might I ask why you're sitting out here and not in the hall?"

"No, you may not, because you should already know why."

"I won't play this childish game of back and forth with you, Nevaeh. Why aren't you at the ball?"

"I don't wish to be in a room where I was publicly made a fool of. Where I feel uncomfortable and unwanted. Bad enough I must live with that feeling every day with you, but to do it in front of strangers? That's something I will not do."

"And how have I made you feel that way? I've been nothing but courteous to you even when I didn't want to, and at the end of the day Nevaeh, you have a duty—" he begins, his tone strained before Nevaeh finally turns to him with fury. "—no, *you* have a duty as King. I have no formal ties to you or any faction of this realm. I will not be openly mocked by a man who cannot properly display his emotions and better yet, admit when he's wrong."

Damien walks up to her then, his eyes wild as he pointed down at her.

"Emotions, huh? You speak so highly of emotions like you know everything there is to know about them. Though, you know nothing of how I feel or why I act as I do because everything that I've ever done in this lifetime has been with reason and for the betterment of this realm."

"Betterment of this realm? What better things have you done, Damien? Besides instill fear and pain in patrons and tell your loyal subjects that you have matters under control when you clearly don't."

She stands, wavering for a moment before regaining her balance. She stands straight, looking at Damien's piercing green eyes as she waited for his next onslaught of words.

"You know just how to get under my skin and pierce my core." He says, nearly breathless as he nears her once more. He cautiously reaches up towards her neck, his hand ghosting over her pulsing flesh as he watched her chest rise and fall with each strained breath.

"I want to hate you, Nevaeh. I really do, but I can't. You...you've helped me find a part of myself I didn't know existed anymore. I didn't think I could feel…" He whispers, his voice wavering before he shuts in eyes in anguish. He sighed, opening them to see Nevaeh wide eyed and awaiting his next onslaught of words.

"I've never apologized for anything I've done in my entire life. Though, I've seen how negatively my words have affected you since the last time we last spoke. I hope that you can find it within yourself to somehow forgive me for the things that I have said, as they were not a direct representation of how I feel for you, but rather, a representation of the fear I felt once I realized these feelings—that they were feelings that I cannot have for you. I am dangerous, this place is dangerous…the people outside this citadel, they do not have your best interest." He finally places his hand on her throat, his touch immediately sending chills over Nevaeh's body as she was frozen in place. She softly places her hand on his wrist, the action making him close his eyes as he shook his head lightly.

"I've been selfish my whole life, Nevaeh. There's nothing that I wanted that I never received. I was supposed to marry but I didn't because like you, I didn't want to be frivolous—I wanted my love to be reciprocated genuinely. I thought it would never happen because I've been numb inside for years. Nevaeh… I wish you could find a means to be happy here, so we might find a way to build a relationship. I've been the one in denial this whole time. I was so combative because it's who I am; I'm selfish. I blamed Medici and Davina for pushing me to get close, but in all honesty, secretly, I longed for a connection. I *want* you to stay forever with me. I *want* you to build a life here, with me. Though, I've come to realize that I cannot continue to be angry with you if you really believe that this is a place you cannot call home. We're from two very different worlds, Nevaeh. It's time we start being honest with one another and our actions."

"You don't hate me?" she asked lowly, barely audible.

Damien smirked, a curt chuckle slipping past his curved lips as he found it amusing, that was the statement that came to mind after his heartfelt confession. He gently traced the outline of her lips, his brows tugging together in a mix of contempt and longing as he answered her lowly, "Not by a longshot."

"Then what?" She asks carefully, her chest feeling like it was closing by the second.

"Then you must go."

"What about the prophecy? We cannot undo what's already been done." She states, her eyes pleading as he gives a trying smile.

"Well, the bond hasn't been completed yet. Besides, the book was written once and can, and will be, written again a thousand times over."

Her brows tugged together in confusion, stepping away from him before she questioned him.

"What do you mean it hasn't been completed?"

He nodded once, motioning for her to walk towards the gazebo so they could sit. Once they were settled, Damien cleared his throat and began with a sigh.

"The bond. It was written that an angel, with a name mirroring her realm, would fall from heaven to hell and wed its ruler. It was both a curse and lesson, and it happens once every thousand years. It was the result of the actions of a selfish King who left Hell to live selfishly amongst the people of Earth. He left behind his wife, unhappy with their relationship after a fight. So, he went to earth in attempts to get away from the royal life and instead fell in love with a human. This woman would become pregnant following their brief encounter, but the King was unaware of this until years after the fact."

"What happened next? Did the Queen ever find out about the child?"

"Well, yes. Satan could not understand how we could be in love with two women simultaneously. He went back to Earth a few years after his first visit, following the news that he was to welcome a son with his queen. He searched for his earth love, but ended up finding an extra human he did not anticipate. She told him the child was his, and his moral compass urged him to take responsibility for the young. He instead went back to Hell, torn apart, ashamed that he had a child with a human before his own Queen. Though Satan enjoyed the chaos, so he admitted his actions to the queen. Legend says she argued with Satan to bring the child to the realm, so that their son might have a sibling to grow up with. He agreed upon debating, and he made a secret trip to Earth and took the child in the night. The council was not happy about this situation, as having relationships outside one's bloodline is strictly forbidden. They made plans to kill the child. They couldn't risk her potentially leaving and outing the court and the very existence of Hell."

Nevaeh shook her head, her brows tugging together as she opened her mouth to speak but nothing came out. She took a beat, then spoke.

"They killed the child. Why would they do that?"

"They didn't. The Queen proposed an alternative."

Damien cleared his throat, leaning forward as he rested his elbows on his knees. Nevaeh was frozen in place, her eyes leveled as she anticipated his answer.

"She decided that a child's life was precious and more important than a set of laws or social guidelines. So, to pay for her husband's ultimate sin and to protect the life of an innocent child, she gave her life to the council instead."

"What? Wasn't she pregnant? What happened to the baby?"

"She had her son, but after the birth they slaughtered her in the main courtyard of the citadel as an example to all. Not even the royal subjects are above the rules of the realm."

"Okay, so she was murdered. How can a council kill their own Queen? How did the prophecy come into play? I don't understand any of this."

"Right, and well, according to the legend, Satan was disgraced with himself enough to seek out the overseer and request for his wife's life to be reinstated and instead he be the one to die. The overseer declined his request, stating that her death was a direct consequence of his action but instead offered him an alternative. Instead of living with the pain of losing his wife, the overseer would grant him the opportunity to leave and live life on Earth with the woman he fell in love with, but his two children would have to stay behind and each of their memories be erased of them. As if that weren't enough, the overseer declared that every thousand years, there would be a bond curse put in place to disrupt the order of the realms and the only way to stop the destruction of the realms would be for the two parties to fall in love completely and genuinely with one another. If they don't, there would be uncharted war amongst the realms, including Earth."

Nevaeh's eyes widen, nodding to herself a few times before her caught the gaze of Damien.

"So there really is no way around this, huh. Its literally do or die."

"I wouldn't say that, but everyone's life would become very dysregulated."

"So, everyone is affected? There's no neutral ground."

"Unfortunately, not. Seems like no one really gets out alive of this one."

Nevaeh looks down at her hands, her brain hurting from all the new information she just received. She closes her eyes, trying to steady her breathing before looking down before Damien's low voice brought her back to reality.

"You said it before, remember? You'll create your own destiny, no matter what. As much as I can try, I cannot stop you from doing what you believe is right."

"The prophecy, though. If I stay and love you, this will all be over. The pain, the war on the realms…we can make a difference and stop the pending carnage, Damien. After that night at the pavilion, I know…I know we said a lot of hurtful things but what you're saying…that really can't be what you want?"

"What is it that I want, Nevaeh?" He counters deeply, his eyes raking over her timid frame as she shook her head in protest. Her eyes were glassy, her voice hoarse as she tried to keep her tears and emotions at bay but failed tremendously.

"You want me to stay, Damien. You said it yourself…you want me to be your queen, to rule beside you. To…to take all your books out of your library and hoard them in my room just so you can order people to accommodate for space. You need me here to keep you talking because you've gone days without uttering a word to anyone but to yourself in your head. You need me here to…to stay up late and to laugh with. I'm…I need to…" she begins to trail off, his face twisting in longing and sadness as he stands and carefully walks over to her seated position. He kneels on one knee, softly grabbing her hand in his.

"You need to find your way, no matter what an old book says. You never meant to come to Hell, this wasn't your desired destination. So, I will help you get to where you need to be." He finishes, releasing her as he stands and steps backward with a ghost of a smile.

Nevaeh sat in place, frozen and deliberately longing for his touch once more. She held onto her tears, blinking them away as she looked down at the deep red color of her bodice instead of his green eyes. "You'll be putting the realm in danger for me. You would risk putting everyone in danger just to let me go?" she asks lowly, looking at the dense green hedge and avoiding Damien's eyes.

Damien watched her, gauged her reaction before giving a trying smile and looking backward toward the castle.

"I would really appreciate your company at the ball. If you could at least come back for the Waltz…it would save me a lot of damnation from Davina."

Nevaeh finally allowed her smile to show as she nodded once in answer.

"Would you prefer I wait for you?" He asked lowly, his tone making Nevaeh shiver as she shook her head.

"No need, we can go now."

CHAPTER 22

NIGHTSHADE

THE EXCITABLE ATMOSPHERE OF the hall was mingled with underlying feelings of curiosity as Damien and Nevaeh continued to mingle through the room as a pair. The angel met many of Hell's elites, including division leaders and council members alike. Nevaeh kept her cup full for the evening, sipping from the dark liquor once or twice to adhere to societal norms. An hour or so had passed since the duo reentered the party, the guests becoming more liberated as time seemed to pass and the liquor kept flowing. Even Damien seemed more relaxed, his first few buttons of his shirt undone to reveal a slim black gold chain enraptured in tiny emeralds. It glistened underneath the dim light when he moved a certain way, the light catching her eyes each time. She carefully touched her collarbone, her heart skipping a beat as she suddenly remembered the absence of her necklace from Damien. Upon realization, she began to delve into a world of her own.

Her thoughts kept jumbling together, her mind playing back the events that have occurred in the past few days—everything that's been said. It didn't make sense, the way Damien seemed so fond of her to then becoming so enraged, then to being completely passive to their situation enough to help her leave Hell for good. It made her brows knit together in confusion; her mind not focused on her current social obligation until she heard a piercing scream rip through the air. She dropped her drink in an instant from being startled, the deep red wine splashing to the ground as realization hit her. Damien held onto her, his arm immediately snaking around her waist to push her behind him amid the chaos. One of the elites held his scorched hand in agony, his skin blistering badly as he began to bleed from the intensity of the burn. Medici pushed through the sea of people, rushing to aid the man as people began to push farther away from Damien and Nevaeh, who still held onto one another. Medici called for some of the guards to escort the wounded elite to the infirmary before clearing his throat and clasping his hands together.

"You may or may not have already known, but, uh, the lovely Nevaeh Azrael, your potential queen becoming, has what you might call the touch of fire. If she is frightened, overwhelmed, etcetera, and or you touch her without consent…you'll be horribly burned. So, let's keep that in mind while we continue this extravaganza, yes? Alright, perfect! Oz, music!"

Just as the music plays and the party begins to flourish once more, disaster strikes again. The golden doors open once more, revealing a line of men dressed in tough leather ensemble. Their faces were adorned with a multitude of lacerations and scars. Each of them had one noticeable gash that was stapled closed with thick metal staples. It made even the hardest of elites back away in terror as they lined up at the entrance of the hall. Damien immediately looked to Dante, who went to round his guards up for the worst. Damien held onto Nevaeh rather tightly by her waist, her hand claiming the lapel of his suit jacket in a mix of fear and anxiousness.

Through the doors, a beautiful woman flanked by another began to make their entrance into the hall. They brought a caliginous energy as they walked in, it was as if every life-form they passed began to diminish with each step forward. The woman walking front and center, Morana, was a sight to behold as she made her dramatic entrance. She was the personification of beauty, dressed in a plunging nude lace gown adorned with a multitude of cascading rubies that fit her like a glove. It looked as though she wore nothing, the rubies reminiscent of blood and its spatter. Her long dark hair cascaded down her back, covering her otherwise bare back to the guests around her. Her icy blue eyes never left Damien's, her walk becoming more meaningful the closer she came until she was prompted to stop by the flooding line of the stygian guard and Dante. She gave a guttural yet flirty laugh as she leveled her eyes with Dante.

"Dante."

"Morana."

"I see you still harbor ill feelings towards me, even after all this time."

"I would've had to care to harbor any feelings, witch."

She chuckles, her eyes flicking over to Damien and finally to Nevaeh. Her whole face fell at the sight of them holding one another, the anger settling in rather quickly before she covered it with a smug smile. Damien released Nevaeh, keeping her behind him as he braced Morana. He kept his hands behind his back, standing tall as he breathed a bit unsteadily. He shook his head in amusement, knowing it was Nevaeh's lack of cool that made him this way. He closed his eyes and tried to steady his heartbeat, almost trying to suppress Nevaeh's anxiety.

"Sorry, I can't help it." She uttered, so low that only Damien could register her words.

Morana stopped a foot away from the duo, her right hand Miako flanking her right side. Morana looked them both over, her plump lips curving upward into a smirk before speaking.

"What a welcoming party, I expected nothing less from the austere King of Hell."

She walks forward, Damien gripping Nevaeh's side as she shuddered at Morana's proximity. She circled the pair, looking them up, down, and over as she leveled her eyes with the frightened guests around them. She reaches outward, smoothing her hand along Damien's shoulder and down his back before allowing a soft chuckle to pass her red painted lips.

"Oh, Damie, how I missed you. I figured my letters got lost in the mail, so I had to show face."

"Speaking of mail, did you receive my gift? I made sure it was sent express and with gratitude."

Morana grimaced, the anger settling in her eyes as she looked over at Nevaeh ruefully.

"This is the reason why I was sent a bloody valentine?" She said rather playfully, walking right up to Nevaeh with a smug smile. She breathes in deeply, closing her eyes before exhaling dramatically.

"Mmm, I can smell the absolute fear radiating from you. So, what's so special about you that would make a cold-hearted monarch send a nearly unidentifiable soldier to my doorstep with a threatening letter tied with a fucking bow?"

Nevaeh raises her chin slightly up at her, clenching her jaw before leveling her eyes with Morana.

"I'm all ears. Don't worry I won't bite…yet."

"That's enough, Morana," Damien interjects strongly, causing her to step back smoothly.

"What's the matter baby? What kind of potential queen of Hell can't take the heat?"

"You know you and your ragtag team aren't welcome here, you're banished by extension of treason to the crown."

"Treason?! Funny you talk of treason, while you're shacked up with an Angel."

The gasps from the crowd around them made Nevaeh jump in surprise. Morana's eyes glittered in delight as she laughed.

"I mean, come on, isn't it obvious? She hasn't a bad bone in her frail little body. It's against the law to fornicate with others outside your realm bloodline. Seriously, you of all people should know that—"

What happened next had the entire room frantic and in a screaming match. Damien reached forward and grabbed Morana by her throat in a fit of rage. It sent everyone into a frenzy, as the entirety of the stygian guard and renegade division faced off. Morana and Damien stared at one another closely, both of their anger brewing dangerously as they saw the potential fight around them. Miako held her sword right to Damien's neck as Dante had his own weapon drawn right under Miako's chin. One strong move on either of their parts would ring deadly.

"How I missed your hands around my neck—" Morana whispers sultrily, before he squeezes harder, making everyone move an extra inch in anticipation.

"—enough of your childish antics, Morana. Now leave."

"She won't be good for you, Damien. Deep down in your blackened heart, you know that for a fact. It's exactly why you're gonna let her go."

Damien releases his grip from Morana's throat, causing her to gasp and cough from the lack of oxygen. Miako immediately places herself in front of a gasping Morana as Dante does the same for Damien and Nevaeh. Once she regains her composure, Morana begins to laugh almost maniacally. "Oh, you know how to get a party going, Damien. I'll go, but I'm not leaving without a dance. So…" She pushes past Miako and up to a stoic Damien.

"I'd start dancing." She almost spits before Damien looks over to Medici's frantic state. He nods, giving him the okay to start the Waltz. Medici instructs Oz to start the music as he announces the start to the guests to nervously take position. Nevaeh looks to Damien in surprise as he takes Morana's hand.

"Damien—" She begins but is quickly stopped by his sharp words.

"I need you to step back."

His words sent her tumbling backwards into a nearby pillar where Medici found her almost instantly. The overflowing tears in her eyes blurred her vision as she watched Damien take stance to dance with Morana. Medici did his best to comfort her, talking to her nonstop as they began to dance the routine she practiced so diligently for. Her vision was blurry from the tears, but she continued to watch the pair glide across the floor. The feeling she currently felt was so brand new, so raw, it sent her skin a flame. She started to breathe erratically, her hands balling into fists beside her as she slowly looked over to see Medici, Lennox, and Davina—all with worried and frustrated faces.

That's when she realized what she was feeling. She was jealous and absolutely enraged at the sight before her. Morana kept her body glued to Damien's as they floated through the routine, her sickeningly sweet smile enough to send Nevaeh into a murderous fit. She kept whispering into his ear, her narrowed gaze meeting Nevaeh's blurry ones from across the room. Her hands moved slowly over his shoulders and down the sides of his back, her lips pulling upwards into a smirk before she careened her slender digits into the nape of his neck. The dip was coming, Nevaeh nearly breathless as she prayed Morana wouldn't do what she thought she would do in that moment. When the moment came, it was fleeting, with Damien dipping Morana briefly before he set her upright again. It wasn't until he went to pull away from her hands was when she tugged him inward for a sickeningly sweet kiss that had her wrapping her arms around his shoulders in bliss.

Nevaeh couldn't help the gasp that slipped past her lips, the accompanying hot tears that fell from her eyes was enough to get her far away from the room. She rushed out of the ballroom, rushing away from the sea of people to solace. She continued to cry, the image of Morana embracing Damien in such an intimate way had her in such pain. She never thought that she could feel like this, the idea becoming pushed away as soon as it entered her mind. Though why would she push it away? *Shouldn't I want this?* She thought, her vision blurry as she quickly stumbled down the steps towards the garden hedge entrance.

Before she made it down, a figure appeared at the side of the garden's entrance. Nevaeh stopped suddenly, her chest heaving as she tried to see through the thick hedge and warm light of the fire pots that illuminated the space.

"Who's there?" she called, her voice wavering before she cleared her throat.

The figure chuckled, stepping forward slowly as Nevaeh stepped back in answer, tripping on her gown which sent her falling straight on her bottom on the stairs.

"Don't come any closer!" She exclaimed to the hooded figure, who stopped immediately upon her request. Nevaeh watched the figure cautiously, her eyes wide as she tried to take in as much of the scene as possible. The mysterious figure reached up then, clutching the black fabric of the hood before pulling it back and away from their head. Nevaeh gasped, her hand immediately flying up to her mouth in a mix of bewilderment and curiosity.

It was a man, he was taller than most, probably about six-foot-five, his limbs and physical appearance rather gaudy and alien like. He was extremely thin, his face gaunt, his eyes milky white. He smiled and it was terrifying, it took up the entirety of his face with what looked like razor-sharp teeth. His mouth was rather shark-like, Nevaeh noted almost immediately.

"Mssssssssssssssss. Nevaeh Azrael," the man spoke, his voice high pitched and very inhuman to the ears.

It sent Nevaeh upright, fumbling to get back on her feet before the man stepped forward again. She froze, watching his next move, before he placed his arms out around him for theatrics.

"A little hellion told me that you're in need of my services. To what do I owe the pleasure?"

Nevaeh shook her head, her throat dried suddenly as she shook from fear.

"Who are you?"

"Me? Why, I'm everything, everywhere, sometimes even all at once. Who are you?" He inquired, his head dipping downward and tilting to get a better view of the fearful angel before him.

"What do you want from me?!" She exclaimed, causing the man to place his hand over his chest with a mocking frown.

"Me? I don't want anything from you, my dear. For it is I who has come to dutifully serve you. I hear you want to travel someplace less...*chaotic*, yes?""How do you know about that?" She spat instantly, the man covering his mouth in mock amusement.

"Oh, dear. Remember? Everything, everywhere, and some-times..." he looks at her, his smile spreading wickedly as he took a few steps forward in quick succession, so he towered over Nevaeh.

"...all at once." He finished gruffly, Nevaeh closing her eyes as he stepped back.

"My, my, little angel, have you forgotten? Is Earth not a priority anymore? I thought I was coming to help you, though if you're set on remaining in place—"

"—*no!*" Nevaeh exclaimed, her breath catching as she surprised herself with her over-zealous reply.

The man smiled widely again, turning his back to her as he walked into the open area of the courtyard before turning to face her again.

"Shall we then?" He called expectedly.

It was then that Nevaeh felt that the world became narrow, her senses heightened as she stood to her feet shakily. This was it; this is the moment she's been waiting for ever since she fell into this realm nearly a year ago. She carefully stepped down, walking slowly but carefully towards the obscure looking man in the center of the courtyard. With a few feet between them, the man hummed, walking toward her, and circling her like prey.

"What do you want from me?"

He guffaws, making the angel jump in surprise.

"Oh, sweet angel Nevaeh. I don't need much from you. Just a small piece of your lifeline—" he growls, grabbing her wrist strongly which only elicited a piercing scream from Nevaeh before she screamed in something other than fear. Pain. The man had sliced her wrist open, her blood spilling onto the concrete below them in a mix of spatter patterns as Nevaeh pulled away from the man who began laughing uncontrollably. She held onto her wound tightly, her blood smeared over her arms and face in a rather macabre sight. She stumbled a bit, her blood dripping from her wrist even with the tight grip she had on it. The man never ceased laughing, the sound making her ears ring as he moved his hands in a circular motion before pushing them forward to reveal a circular and electric looking portal. It sparked and glowed a violent mix of red and blue, the inside a rapid swirl of color and light.

The man hunched over, looking over at a stumbling Nevaeh as he reached forward and grabbed her by the hair. She shouted in protest, releasing her grasp on her wrist to place her hands in the fistful of hair in the man's hand. He pulled her close to the circular void, holding her outward so he could see her blood-stained face, full of fear. Right as the man was about to speak to her, a new voice broke through the otherwise heinous silence.

"NEVAEH!"

It was Damien, along with Dante and the entire stygian guard. The man knew what was coming next, the stygian creatures racing over in lightning speed. Nevaeh's eyes widened, the man roughly turning her around, so her back was to his front. He laughed again, stooping abruptly to whisper sinisterly in her ear, "Morana sends her regards".

It happened so quickly; Nevaeh felt as if she had the air knocked out of her lungs. He had pushed her forward forcefully, her body twisting so she faced the evil man and the onslaught of stygian guards who immediately jumped his bones. She could hear him, right as the portal closed and right before everything went black—she heard him. She wouldn't ever forget the sound, the complete sadness and even fear in the tone. It was Damien, screaming for her, and for her alone.

EPILOGUE

Division Three // The Renegades

The putrid smell of blood and smoke made a disheveled Cassius Blake nearly vomit as he rested against a thick oak tree just outside of Division Three of Hell. He could faintly make out the small specs fire that seemed to line the entrance around the tall wall of the city, the smoke streamed steadily from its respective posts up into the deep navy sky above. Cassius groaned, his eyes red from the smoke and smell, but he stumbled forward still. His body felt heavy, his neck still stinging and tense from his means of making it into the realm. He cleared his throat, bringing his forearm up and over his nose as he tried to acclimate himself to the horrid smell as he ventured closer. Cassius slowed his pace once he got close enough to the tall wall, it seemed to extend for an eternity on either side of him.

It was both intriguing and frightening to see what appeared to be metal welded in such a way. Rust and grime riddled the material, dark streaks and speckled blood lined the lengths of the wall. Cassius closed his eyes in disgust, coughing in response to the fire sources lining the lengths of the wall. Heads, burning heads on spears—Cassius couldn't believe his eyes. He turned away, doubling over as he emptied the contents of his stomach on the muddled black soil and branches under his feet.

Cassius heaved, his body shaking slightly as he tried to regain his composure after vomiting rather violently. His blood shot eyes peered up again and over his shoulder at the malicious looking entrance of Hell's division three sector. It was as if something deep inside of him compelled his body forward rather quickly, his feet not swift enough as he fell to his knees. Cassius continued to breathe raggedly, his fingertips digging deeply into the dark soil and ash. He gathered himself for a moment, groaning as he rose to his feet again. He wavered slightly, moving forward towards the entrance. Upon venturing closer, Cassius could hear piercing screams and laughter; sounds that did not sound at all inviting. He continued despite his gut telling him to stop, his boots crunching against the ominous mix of dirt, gravel, and bone as he made it across the entrance threshold. He coughed a few times, a heavy inhabitance of smoke now apparent in the air around him as he looked out towards what seemed to be a bustling but rather menacing village. The sky above was a deep red and orange, the smoke canvassing the entire area like the plague. Cassius continued to cough, forearm going up to shield his nose before he ventured forward into the population.

The smell was much worse inside the populus, Cassius' eyes teared up immediately as he stopped himself multiple times from gagging. Burning and rotting flesh, blood, and smoke intertwined and created a hellish and rather unbearable scent to anyone else other than a division three native. He walked past many tents and tables, something similar of a market, as he continued his path through the city. His head began to throb, his vision became splotchy for a moment before a sharp pain in his head sent him crashing into a table besides him. A fleeting scene flashed before his eyes; the environment almost identical to where he was currently. The vision sent him flying forward, the image of a red door bright behind his closed eyes as that melodic voice called again. Cassius' eyes shot open once again, a myriad of disturbed and distorted faces came to view as some of the hellions peered over Cassius' limp body. Cassius exclaimed in sheer fear, the creatures backing away cautiously as Cassius stood again. He kept his hands out in attempts to seem unlike a threat, though the hellions immediately knew he was misplaced. His clothing and behavior gave him straight away.

"Excuse me, I'm looking for a red door. An establishment with a red door," he asked hastily, his eyes frantic as he watched the hellions laugh and gawk at him. Some just stared on in what might have been curiosity or feigned indifference. Upon hearing no answer, Cassius continued. He trudged through the wet earth; taken back by the cruelties and lewd activity he was witnessing out in the open and without care. He averted his eyes ahead, trying his best to drown out the obscenities around him as he occasionally looked about for a red door. His chest ached suddenly, sending him crashing into a deteriorating pilar as he clutched at the fabric covering his chest. His eyes rolled back into his head, his forehead beading with sweat as he struggled to breathe. He coughed, the action making him double over as he spat a mouthful of blood onto the rather decimated concrete below him. He looked at it in a mix of fear and bewilderment, unsure as to why he could be coughing up such dark looking blood. The color was almost the shade of molasses, nearly black. He looked up and around, about to continue his journey before he stopped in his tracks.

A lone light shined in a slim alleyway just opposite where he stood, he could see just a corner of what he was looking for all this time. Unsure, he willed himself forward and towards the small entrance of the side street. He went forward slowly, his shaking hands claiming the hot concrete of the deteriorating building as he slid sideways to get into the secluded area. It was almost black; Cassius was at a loss for words of how the lighting shifted so greatly. Once he shimmed his way through, he looked up at the sky again, but this time was greeted with a black abyss. He looked behind him, the small alleyway giving forth a dense red-orange glow of the main city. He looked back again, now towards the almost shiny red door just feet before him. A singular bright white light illuminated the entrance. He stepped carefully, his feet splashing into the unseen pools of blood that lined every street in division three. He climbed the stone steps slowly, his eyes wide as he couldn't believe that the visions were real. His fist rose inches from knocking before he heard a low and sinister voice. It was grave and raspy, it sounded threatening and almost inhuman. He froze, his body shaking slightly as he carefully turned his head around to the darkness surrounding him. Cassius could hear his heart beating, his blood pumping rapidly. He called out unsteadily, "Who's there? Show yourself!"

Silence was his answer, the moment lasted long enough for Cassius to turn back around and go to knock again before his fist stopped mid-rise to meet the red lacquer of the door once again. Every hair on his back stood up on end, his blood running cold at the sound of a low and forbidding growl and clicking sound. His breath caught in his throat, frozen in place as he listened. The words uttered from behind him did not sound like words, the language sounded chilling to his ear. Cassius didn't find the strength in him to move or scream until he felt pressure on his right shoulder. He slowly peered over, tears spilling over as he registered decaying pointed fingers gripping the dirtied fabric of his jacket before everything went completely dark.

www.ingramcontent.com/pod-product-compliance
Lightning Source LLC
Chambersburg PA
CBHW050321160726
48002CB00001B/136